Deck of Tales

A Speculative Fiction Anthology

Book Cover and Illustrations by J.J.MONGK

Table of Contents

The Cup of Noodles

Margaret Lê

Alameda County Nourishment Center
Intake Form

Form A-500D
DateTime: February 23, 2165 09:35a PST
Have you felt hungry in the last 24 hours?
☐ Yes ☐ No
Have you felt overly full in the last 24 hours?
☐ Yes ☐ No
What color is your health monitor?
☐ Red ☐ Pink ☐ Orange ☐ Yellow ☐
Green
Are you receiving any supplemental
medications in your nourishment bank?
☐ Yes ☐ No
Please connect your health monitor to
proceed.

***

"Good morning Mx. Tran."

I hear Baco grunt. Yet, despite the "hrmph," her eyebrows, aged 120 years, don't budge.

Welp, this is different. Switching my monitor to record. There's a slight chance today's "Take your Baco on an errand" agenda is going to make for shareable content, providence permitting. For folks at home, they are discreetly leading Baco and I into a back room. To catch you all up, five minutes ago, Baco linked up her health monitor to the nourishment kiosk. Instead of getting her nourishment bank replenished, the kiosk's lights twinkled ever so slightly. Most folks would have missed it, unless for some reason, you were keyed in on an ancient Vietnamese woman and her ethnically ambiguous, yet very handsome, great-grandson (duh, me). Now, we're walking down a bland hallway following an equally bland-looking proctor who earlier wiggled his finger at us to follow him in a classic villain way. His name tag reads: Mx. Smith-Visharyan (he/him).

The room reminds me of a scene from those ancient law enforcement television series, the kind that existed before hyper-color capture. Talk about drab. The walls are a light-gray paint. If I were a paint namer, I'd call it, "gobsmacked gray." This color needs all the marketing help it can get. In cliché fashion, there's an aluminum desk made to look like steel in the middle of the room. Clearly, money is no object. A heavy sigh would knock it over.

The desk is bare save for the proctor's hands which are clasped, lightly resting on top. He makes Baco sit on a chair on one side of the desk, and he settles his cold-eyed-enforcer butt on the twin chair on the opposite side. He orders me to the corner outside of the conversation bubble, like a toddler left with a digi-crayon and project easel, away from adult talk. Check out this sea of info-guides.

The bubble's distortion cloud and white noise challenge my eavesdropping abilities, but don't completely erase years of finely tuned perception proficiencies. *Yes, I'm a nosy busybody.* Yet, it is effectively putting the kibosh on my content recording. **Max, the time is now 14:00. You have been immobile for 15 minutes now. If unable to briskly walk, try a few minutes of in-place calisthenics.** My life monitor is chastising me. Welp, I've officially been babysitting Baco for two hours—two hours I could've spent creating usable content.

I turn my attention back to my immediate surroundings. What is this corner they have me banished to? It's like a waiting room had a baby with a propaganda machine. The info-guides are inset into the walls. Dynamic interactive

7

information displays touting the global benefits of nourishment banks scream at me everywhere I turn. The one straight in front of me wants to know if I know that "… before we installed nourishment technology across the planet, 50% of all habitable land was used for agriculture?" Yes, of course I did. Learned that in primary school, thank you very much.

I swipe up.

Ooh, now what?

I'll tell you what—a friendly animated dancing anthropomorphic earth sings, "Congratulations! YOU are doing your part to eradicate the global housing crisis." Geez. C-content, banking on a captive audience.

"When was the last time you had your nourishment bank refilled Mx. Tran?"

Is that Mx. Smith- Visharyan's getting loud with Baco? There's frustration and, dare I say, anger swirling in the increased volume.

"Two munts," Baco volleys back. Go Baco!

"Two months? That's a long time. Any reason for not coming in last month? We ask that people try to keep to a monthly visit to ensure our population is in tip-top shape."

I try to inch closer, but being surreptitious is

not my greatest strength.

"Sit a-roun' too much. Only small hunger. Very ol' lady."

That old shriv liar.

Baco isn't idle. I have never seen her sitting down. She is forever running around doing something or other. At least that's been the case since I've known her. Though it has been a while since I've spent time with her. Keeping up with the feeds and building my brand is more taxing than people think, and coming up with new content ideas is all I have time for these days.

"That's exactly why you should be coming, Mx. Tran. We can continue to check your activity and properly regulate the necessary changes to your nourishment bank if you keep your health monitor online. But for some reason, we're not seeing consistent data from your body feeds."

I'm getting pretty good at eavesdropping through their conversation bubble. One more superpower to add to my list. Mental note, my body feeds could be a goldmine for content.

"No need. Health-ee. Jus' layzee. Come here is too much trouble."

"You ARE fine, Mx. Tran. In fact, you're in wonderful shape based on the health scan we ran as you came through the door. You are unusually fine for someone who has not visited the nourishment bank in two months. Our health scan reads your muscles are that of a 75-year-old, if that. You're as healthy as someone half your age. However, you DO need nourishment. You NEED it because it's the law and you NEED it so that you can continue to be in good health, but more importantly, you NEED to be a good citizen, Mx. Tran. Don't you WANT to be a good global citizen Mx. Tran?"

What's the deal with Mx. Smith Visharyan and his oversized reaction to Baco's dainty sustenance needs? What a tool!

"No need to come here if you sign up for automated replenishment."

"I keep trying to tell her that, Mx. Smith-Visharyan. She doesn't trust the automated replenishment system."

Mx. Smith-Visharyan shifts his whole body and the metal chair around to look at me. He touches a bunch of buttons on his display and the conversation bubble lowers. "Mx.

Tran-Diop, this is supposed to be a private conversation. We allowed you in the room as a courtesy to your great-grandmother. Are you here as an official representative for her?"

"Uh, not really. I just agreed to accompany her because she hates riding in autopods by herself, and if I'm being honest, my mom asked me to."

"Are you familiar with her lifestyle habits and why she hasn't been complying with government nourishment mandates?"

"I am not. I seldom see my great-grandmother these days and, as you can see, she barely speaks English, so our relationship is pretty shallow. I don't speak Vietnamese."

"I appreciate your transparency, Mx. Tran-Diop."

"Yeah, well, it's sorta my brand. Maybe you've peeped my channel on one of the feeds? *A Day in the Life of that Man Tran, Max Tran-Diop.*"

Did I just catch him rolling his eyes at me?

As if confirming my uselessness, Mx. Smith-Visharyan turns his metal chair all the way back around towards Baco, but this time, he doesn't raise the conversation bubble. "Mx. Tran, I'm going to ask you again. Why has it been so long since you've visited a nourishment bank?"

"I tole you before. Slow lifesty'. Too much hassle."

"You understand that monthly banks are not optional. Law mandates them."

"I don' understand. Not how was."

"The law has been in effect for nearly a decade, and your noncompliance has been consistent for years."

Baco's calm face looks defiant. Now what's this guy doing? He keeps looking down at the monitor, mouthing words at the display, and nodding to whoever might be watching us. And now the lights dim. What the actual eff? Shadowy, heavily armed figures appear from the room's corners, as if they had been there all along. Now Mx. Smith-Visharyan shifts and stares straight at me.

"I was hoping this was a matter we could settle quickly today, Mx. Tran-Diop, but Mx. Tran has been uncooperative, and you've been less than helpful. This is a matter of great seriousness. We have reason to believe that your great-grandmother is willfully engaging in subversive and treasonous behavior, and we must detain her for further questioning. If there is someone more familiar with her circumstances who can assist in this matter, I advise you to get in contact with them."

"I don't understand. Isn't this a nourishment center? Shouldn't you just be refilling her bank and letting us get on with our day?"

"Mx. Tran-Diop, we are a government agency—one that ensures that our population and planet remain healthy. We do this by enforcing government regulations and upholding the values of the Global Nourishment Alliance. Unless you have information that will be helpful to this investigation, my colleagues will escort you out."

Mx. Smith-Visharyan gestures towards the menacing figures in the shadows who are a smidge over armed with their directed-energy weapons slung over their shoulders. I look over at Baco, wiping away the dampness collecting at my throbbing temples and the wetness beginning to pool in the corners of my eyes.

"Should I get mom or ba ngoai?"

"No. Go find my cốc hạnh phúc. Inside everything we need."

Baco's faith in my grasp of Vietnamese is

admirable, but ill placed when we're in dire straits. Pretty much every time I see her, she tries to jump start my Vietnamese, as if it's a jacket I merely misplaced. I've never been able to get the accents down, and it makes me feel sucky. Saying anything in Vietnamese makes me feel stupid and inadequate, so I stopped trying and eventually stopped visiting her so much.

She looks at me with expectant eyes, searching for my familiarity, placing trust in a fractional part of me I haven't felt connected to in years. I give her my best wink, hoping I can find what we need.

***

I run away from the nourishment center, unsure of where I'm going, but needing the rhythm to keep Baco's words in my memory, repeating the words at every step. Jogging amazingly is working. Happy cup! She wants me to find her happy cup, although WTF is a happy cup? Maybe she's got money in it? A number to an attorney? I open up my archive folder. Years ago, I helped Baco organize her live-in unit and

14

documented it for my viewers. Baco content is always popular with my followers. I scan the videos to find all the images of cups. Nothing. I broaden the search to include all my archive videos. Bingo!

Should I turn on my monitor to record? This could be great content. No, stupid. Mx. Smith-Visharyan's colleagues weren't holding fake guns. There's a non-zero possibility the Nourishment Agency might be tracking my movements. I need to be smart about this. As I look up and down the street, I spot an unlicensed autopod tucked in an alley up ahead. Hopping in, I tell the driver to take me to Sylvester's Talent Agency.

I breathe a sigh of relief as the autopod deftly maneuvers through the densely packed airspace. The more crafts filling the airspace, the harder it'll be for anyone to track me. In the distance, I spot a familiar cup plastered across the brick facade on the side of Sylvester's Talent Agency building, growing larger as we approach.

The last time I saw my great-grandmother was a year ago. Mom asked me to pick Baco up from her live-in unit and bring her to dad's 65th birthday party. I felt foolish that day because Mom insisted I wear a boubou, while Dad was adamant I wear an áo gấm. So I was a walking cacophony of ridiculous traditional garb, though it made for quality content. When I picked Baco up, she looked at me and laughed. We rode the autopod, me mostly silent. Baco was staring out the window, smiling, pointing things out. I would nod politely, pretending I knew what she was talking about. I always thought it odd, her broken English, despite having been in the States since she was a kid. For some reason I feel like I understood her better when I was a kid, but as I got older, it seemed her English got worse, until I just gave up trying to understand her.

At one point during that ride, she jabbed me really hard with a stiff index finger to my rib and excitedly pointed out a washed-out advertisement on an older brick building—one of the few that hadn't been demolished for a glass highrise. Baco's tour-guide observation had been insistent, and I looked up from my feed to take note. The advertisement featured a giant hot steaming cup. Hovering above the cup was a pair of chopsticks and dangling from those chopsticks were noodles. The noodles spelled out Lê Vân Yummy Noods in cursive. With eyes sparkling, wet like the imaginary soup in the cup, Baco proclaimed, "Bún bò Huế. That used to be your favorite. Happy, warm cup of noodles."

My favorite? Baco was clearly confused. I'd never eaten anything in my life. The building's entrance came into our view, revealing a glassy frontage illuminated by a brightly lit sign. It read Sylvester's Talent Agency. The abrupt transition from the side of the building to the front had reminded me of the lenticular prints I learned about in art history class, like Lichtenstein's "Fish and Sky." It seemed like two buildings in one.

At the time, Baco remarked, "Maybe some day you be famous like you want, and you need talent agency. Baco wish that for you."

The autopod comes to a halt, jolting me back. The sight of Sylvester's Talent Agency's vibrant signage pulls me out of the past. I shake off the lingering memory and step out onto the pavement. I have no idea what I'm supposed to do next. Baco said I could find help inside the cup. I see a giant reception desk. It's as good a place to start as any. Though now, in this moment, I'm acutely aware that I may not have the talents needed to help Baco out. At the glass desk sits a kempt, comely young person, every hair in the right place. Her style is giving me professional, yet edgy vibes. Her nameplate reads Beatrice O'Shea Jackson (she/her). On the edges of the lobby, there are equally stylish folks of all varieties. I feel like I'm at fashion week or something. If I weren't here to help Baco, I might consider getting representation. Back to the task, Max. It's now or never.

"Hi there, this is going to be a silly question, but I was sent here by my great-grandmother and was told someone here could help."

With an almost imperceptible glance to the right, left, and behind me, Beatrice asks, "Does your great-grandmother have an appointment?" There's a coy lilt to her question. Hinting at something. I've taken some improv classes at university and recognize a "yes, and" prompt when I hear one.

"Uh, yes, yes she does. Her name is Eva Lien Tran."

"One moment while I check."

Beatrice taps her monitor, touches her ear,

and mouths Baco's name towards the monitor, all the while casually scanning the perimeter behind me.

"Yes, I see right here. She's got an appointment with Gene. I'll let them know you're here. Feel free to have a seat."

I look around for somewhere to sit down, but before I can give myself a moment to breathe, someone walks towards me. The someone I guess is Gene. Stitched on Gene's lapel is their name, Gene Diaz (they/them). Gene is my height and wears a long-sleeved button-down. They have their sleeves rolled back revealing two fully tattooed arms. On one arm is a rolling pin, on the other muffin tins next to a piglet. How retro.

"Right this way."

Gene leads me to the elevators. "Before we head down, might I ask how you arrived here today?"

"Unlicensed autopod."

"Excellent."

Inside the elevators, Gene tags their arm monitor and punches some numbers into the keypad next to the elevator buttons. We descend in silence. When the elevator doors open, I am blasted in the face with smells. ALL...OF...THE...SMELLS!

"Where the hell are we?"

"You must be Max."

"How do you know who I am?"

"Your great-grandmother told me all about you. I can only guess they've caught her. Let me take you to her station. I'll try to explain as much as I can. We've got our folks working on an escalation plan."

In front of me, I see steam. Steam coming off of pots. Steam coming off of pans. I hear crackles all around me. I hear splashes. Chop, chop, chop, matching the syncopation of cleavers moving on wooden boards. I watch hands pushing dough balls on marble countertops with a flourish—conducting the symphony. I see things I have only seen in archival footage and old photo galleries. This shouldn't exist anymore. This is not allowed to exist anymore.

"How...is...this...possible?"

"People make it possible. People like Eva. People who remember and are making sure we still remember. Let me make you something to eat while I fill you in."

We walk by clear plastic enclosures that are wet with condensation, housing what I suspect are indoor gardens. The air around the enclosures feels warm and misty and has a light fragrance that I can only describe as fresh and crispy, if fresh and crispy had a smell. It reminds me of the few times I've managed to wake up at sunrise and walk along the grassy side of Lake Merritt. The room itself is surprisingly cool, despite all the heat generated from the induction burners.

We reach a set of stools in an area close to the middle of the gigantic room. This half is divided into thirds, each with 10 stations that contain an induction cooktop with four burners, a double oven, a refrigerator, a set of cupboards, and shelves of cookware. Every station is occupied by at least one individual busily preparing real food. Food that you can actually consume. Food that is made to be chewed, swallowed, digested, and turned into waste. Food that is made from materials that used to occupy more than half of habitable land. Food that is featured in my favorite vintage content. Food that was legislated out of existence in favor of "nourishment" and sustaining an ever-growing population. We're all thinner and more productive now. That's what they call progress.

My mind recalls the messaging on the info-guides at the Nourishment Center. Coercion, propaganda, suppression—all the hallmarks for a quick and successful transition from one way of life to another. How could I have ignored this for so long? How quickly these smells have rearranged my brain.

As Gene pulls two crusty zeppelin shaped loaves out of the oven, they outline how Sylvester's Talent Agency became a front for this giant kitchen. Truth be told, I am having a hard time following the story as I wipe away the saliva seeping out the sides of my mouth. Also, is it normal for bellies to talk? Because mine is surely telling Gene to hurry the eff up and get this delicious looking food in it. The main thing that manages to cling to my brain waves as my senses are being clobbered is that Baco never stopped cooking. When legislation started being put in place, first through eliminating at-home food prep to ultimately eradicating global food consumption, Baco ran an underground supper club, using electric burners she had from the days when she had her own YouTube cooking channel—Eva Eats. She was one of a group of committed resistors dotting the globe. Why am I hearing all this from Gene? Why didn't Baco tell me herself?

Gene smashes a long reed-like stalk. The smell is familiar and makes me want to weep.

"Lemongrass is a scent that I would never want to live without," Gene interrupts his Baco infused Sylvester's Talent Agency history lesson to remark. "It's what makes bún bò Huế flavors so multi-dimensional." So Baco wasn't confused when she said bún bò Huế was my favorite, and I hadn't been hallucinating memories of smells, an overly full belly, and warm body when I was with my Baco. Every time I watched archival footage of food shows, I always had a visceral reaction that I couldn't quite explain.

From behind me, I hear a bang, followed by a boom. I turn around and into the room rush dozens of government officers, faces covered with gas masks. Clouds of yellow smoke billow around them. We are fucked.

I start ducking for cover, but if I'm going to die, it's not going to be on an empty stomach. So, on the way down, I pull down a sandwich

Gene has prepared; the yellow smoke fumes mingle with the twinkle of spices and waft into my nose. The heavy yellow smoke imparts a level of clarity in me that is undeniable. I start chewing. Despite the chaos of humans shrieking and the clattering of pans and glasses making contact with the concrete floor, a sense of peace washes over me. I grind pickled umami between my teeth.

I devour the bánh mì, lemongrass pushing up into my gums, deep-fried tofu crumbling down my shirt, chili seeds stinging the inside of my cheek. I revel at my inexplicable ability to name all these things that were never in my lexicon. My eyes want to close, my body wants to sleep, and I feel heavy.

Just as I am about to give in to the inevitable, I remember something. Me and Baco sitting on stools at a counter not dissimilar to the one I'm lying under. Baco is smiling at me. She's speaking in Vietnamese, and I understand her. We're loud. Not just our talking, but our eating. We're slurping. We're pulling every noodle into our mouth with gusto, chewing in between to let more noodles in. We're tipping the bowls back into our mouths, letting the broth dribble down our chins. She's laughing as she takes a napkin and dabs my chin.

The Daily Lies of the Young God

J.J. Mongk

*Of the grand city, Yanghe, where the river glows
  gold,*
*the young god slithers among the peonies and
  irises: red, pink and yellow, blue.*
*The summer sun glints off her serpentine tail
  of black and olive scales.*
Doing her duty, hands clasped and gait straight,
*appreciating the garden that was built by those
  who donated*
scarlet hair pins, gold, feathers, and jades.
*Yet her gaze stays on the pond, cares not for the
  blooms.*

Did you really let him kill you? I interrupt Older
One's poem lesson, though I am the one who
asked for it earlier. It is sweltering out here, and
I didn't know she would make the poem about
me.

    Yes, Young One, she replies.
    Weren't you scared?
    At the time, yes.
    Were you mad?
    No.
    Not even a little?
    She smiles. Maybe a little, now that you are.
How could I ever live up to her? Not even

27

being mad getting executed like that by the barbarian? Probably had her head chopped off. I never asked how it was done, and still don't want to know.

I slither tediously through this newly built palace garden under the summer sun, pretending to care about these flowers—peonies, or whatever they are called—that she lauded in the poem. The Huiyi ceremonial garment I'm wearing is long and layered, and makes me sweat. The gem-filled Diguan crown sits heavy atop my head. I wish this slither would end soon. I wonder how many times she had to do this when she was still alive. Looking at her now, she looks majestic and at ease.

Would you like me to continue the poem? Older One asks.

No, thank you. I don't think I'd be able to make a poem like you or ever be like you.
Silly Young One. You and I are one.
Yes, technically. We are both gods and connected by the power of the land, and she does look like me, with the scales, the tail and all. But . . .

Not really. You are much, much older, thousands times wiser, much more proper, and majestic.

She is also much, much bigger, like really big. Her humanoid torso fills up half the height of the Long Hall, which is about as tall as four floors of normal buildings in Yanghe, and her snake hip and tail might as well be called endless. I guess the palace was built to fit her when she took the throne long, long ago.

You're the real god of Yanghe. I tell her.

So are you.

I'm just a girl who lived by the river and somehow sidewinded into this palace and was made a god. Somehow folks just keep believing it.

Folks believe in all kinds of absurd stuff like fortune telling, the heavens, elemental colors, eating a mermaid's flesh for immortality. I had to escape the flesh hunters once or twice when I lived by the river, and I don't even have a fish's tail.

Curve the river, carve the hill, and cure the sick. Older One lists the powers that I now wield. *Would you not call that the power of a god?*

Shamans and sorcerers can do those things too. Maybe not the whole river, and the whole hill, but we all borrow power from the land. I would feel more like a god if I could raise the dead. But I'm not doing any of that right now, am I? I'm only parading myself around these bushes and rocks in front of the rich folk.

Showing appreciation to them is an important duty, Young One. The merchants and nobles are the ones who bring in the gold and employ the folks in the city.

I imagine myself conjuring gold and giving it out. Before I was a god, I had seen little enough of it.

We cannot solve everything with magic. We should not disrupt the balance of nature.

How does she know what I am thinking? I pout and resign myself to my apparently very important duty of appreciating rich folk. I continue my slither. At least the pond looks refreshing. I have not seen many of the fish in it before, despite making my living out of the Golden River—the red-scale arowanas, the high-fin banded sharks, the jelly-head orandas.

Look tasty, do they not?

I scowl at Older One. She just smiles.

"My lady, are you well?" Minister Yang asks.

"Yes, we are all right, minister." I am

sometimes so focused on mind-whispering to Older One that I forget there are other people around.

Minister Yang is the chief minister of the palace and close counsel to the god. However, he does not look much like a court official. He looks more like a warrior, big and furry, with the face that's a mix of goat and ox, the body of a tiger and a boar, and with talons for hands. But he is as gentle as he looks scary. He has been the attendant since my predecessor, the previous god of this grand city.

"We were distracted by the lovely sky and the birds," I say. There were no birds, of course, only the supposed spirit of the long-dead goddess that only I can see. I am unsure if I should tell anyone about her. She could be lying about who she is. She could be a malevolent spirit or an ancient demon playing tricks. Or perhaps it's just me losing my mind from the stress of my duty. Not that anybody would believe me. To most of the court, I'm just a muddy girl who sold fish. I rather have Older One by my side, even if she is lying. At least she takes me seriously.

I did, though, ask Minister Yang whether any

of my kinfolk ever became gods in the history of Yanghe. He said he had not seen any records of a serpent-like god, which made Older One seem more like a delusion. But he said there were many accounts of previous gods dreaming of a giant serpent giving guidance.

That does not really mean much. Who hasn't dreamt of giant beasts? I dream of giant fish all the time.

"As long as you are all right, my lady. We can take a rest if you'd like. I'm sure you are not used to being in the sun."

Because I used to live in the mud, of course. "We can keep going, minister. The weather is nice, and the garden is pleasing,"

I lied. Only the fish look tasty.

***

It was spring when I first entered the palace. I was hauling a cart with two mean-looking sturgeons, the Kaluga, up the paved way to the main gate. I had heard the palace officials were looking to buy exotic fish for the garden pond, and I was happy to have their gold.

The palace was vast. The paved drive could

probably fit ten of my carts side by side. I imagined this was what it felt like for a fish to live in the sea. Not that I had ever seen a sea, but I'd been told it was like a river that had no bank. I was sure the sea was much bigger, much more powerful, and much more fierce than any gods.

I slithered on and on, passing structure after structure, pillar after pillar. The carved stones and inlaid woodwork seemed unending. Everything was painted in the same color, vermilion, like the palace's name.

This was from the long-held belief that the elements—wood, fire, earth, and water—were either amplified or subdued by one another. Wood generated fire but overcame earth, earth generated metal but overcame water, and so on. The fire color of the palace was said to overcome the flooding nature of the Golden River, as the fire melted metal (gold) and evaporated water. I couldn't grasp how colors could possibly affect the course of nature. The wolf-folks could not even see color, so their lives must have been disastrous. And the Golden River was not really gold. It was just the sun reflected on the dark river, like a mirror.

But the palace folks do what the palace folks do. It was not my place to deal with the superstitions of the court.

I repeated the pitch for the fish in my head and tried to keep my hair kempt. I didn't want them to think less of me than they already would, given how I looked. I had fallen asleep earlier after I mudded my body and hair—it had been a hot day. And the mud that I used to cool my body happened to be red clay, so I woke up with red hair.

I arrived at the main reception area, where servants and officials bustled right and left. I tried to get their attention, but all of them were too fast and too focused. So I slithered around, looking for someone standing still. I spotted an official in a large black robe, horns on his head, goat-like, reading a scroll.

I reached him and said, "May you be in good health, sir."

He turned and looked at me with his slot eyes.

"Oh, my lady, we were waiting for you," he said.

"What?"

***

I became the god of Yanghe that day, a few harvests ago now. The palace servants dragged me to the bath. They scrubbed, brushed, and dressed me. The next morning, a celebration was held, and I took up the title and the power of the god.

It seems that, on the new year after the year that my predecessor died, a meteor landed in the middle of the palace carrying a scroll of a prophetic poem:

Fire hair melts freezing snow.
Black tail softens hard earth.
Jade scales bring blooming spring.
Black River's guardians (The Kaluga)
submitting.
Yongdi enters the palace
commanding the earth, water, and sky.
Yanghe prospers for millennia.

Everyone was bewildered. No one knew what to make of the scroll for weeks. The heavens never gave its will, not so directly. The will of the heavens always came in the form of some authority reading it from a scroll or writing it on a paper, though always after the fact—"It was the mandate of heaven that brought the downfall of the fourth dynasty and gave rise to the fifth." Or, "The heavens have willed the first dynasty to unite the six states into one." But the scroll from the meteor was different.

It was the meteor scroll Minister Yang was reading when I slithered up with my red hair, black tail, jade scales, and a brace of kalugas.

Many kowtowed to the prophecy that arrived in the meteor, but many also thought it was some kind of conspiracy. In the end, all agreed that whether the meteor was really from the heavens or not, the land would only grant its power to the rightful god and would reject the unfit. All of my predecessors had done exceptional deeds or had extraordinary talents, all had trained to be accepted by the land. I just slithered into the position with a cart of fish.

Now I sit on the Throne with a headache. The sky is dark. The season's rain pours, and thunder roars. The golden river has been steadily rising these autumn months, and so the court convenes in the Long Hall to mitigate the threat of flood.

"The venerated Yongdi." Minister Wa grovels on his webbed feet and hands, in his black minister uniform, wrapping in a water bubble that I conjured to keep him from drying. "May you live a thousand years. This humble subject would like to implore you not to build the levee where the spirit of the ancestral gods' rest."

"Minister Wa, it is imperative that we prevent the flood," I say. "Even if we could evacuate the folks out of the city, the damage and destruction would lead to starvation. Folks will turn to banditry and savagery. Surely our predecessors would not object to that."

"But goddess, it is improper. We would not want to incur the wrath of the ancestral gods and the heavens."

By then, I have realized that the gods are just another servant of a convoluted system and collective beliefs. It was frustrating all the same.

Do not eat him, Young One.

I make a face at Older One. She gestures toward my body, and I realize I have been coiling into a striking pose. I force myself to relax.

They are going to have me stop the flood instead of building the damn levee to prevent it, I say. *And look how that worked out. We now* argue about the tomb of the god who died stopping the flood, when a simple levee would have stopped him from dying. My predecessors are dead. They don't care. There is no ghost and there is no heaven. This stuff is all made up to convince people to do things.

Older One smirks. *Or not do them.*

I scowl. I just realized that I might have offended Older One by saying that ghosts are not real. *I mean If my predecessors are so angry, they should show themselves like you.* I have not yet come to believe in the spirits of the dead despite always having one standing near me. I did once ask if there are any other spirits of the old gods. Older One said she does not know. She has never seen any other spirits.

You have to address their beliefs, Older One says. *The world is complicated, Young One. Ritual and conduct—*

Are irrational.

Are like laws keeping the peace, not only for society but also for the mind. The world is uncertain and terrorful. Everyone is trying to navigate through the world as best as they can. And that sometimes results in—

Delusional thinking.

Certain beliefs and behaviors. You have to speak to their fear.

I sigh. How can she be so kind and patient? These people are driving me crazy.

I turn my attention back to the court. "Minister Wa, we understand, and we do not want to incur the wrath of my predecessors. But let us assure you that my predecessor and all the ancestral gods love the citizens of Yanghe and would rather have us secure all the city's safety than fret overmuch about honoring them."

Minister Wa remains kowtowing, and the rest of the court gives me blank expressions. I may have overcome my image of a muddy fishmonger over the years but having the title and the throne is not enough to go against centuries of ingrained delusion.

I rub my temples and reach out my power to all the lamps in the palace. Speak to their fear and play to their belief, I shall.

Then I squeeze. The lamps' light flutters and blinks. Chatter echoes from all the ministers and the counsels. Even the attendants gasp.

I allow the lamps to burn bright again, now that I set my illusion. "We have counseled with the spirit of the old gods. They would be glad to have the levee built. The power connects us." I say, which is not a lie. Older One may not have been the god who lies in the tombs, but she is still one of the old gods.

The court looks at each other.

"Let's proceed with the levee," I say.

A lady-fox counsel cuts through the chatter. "What about the heavens, goddess? They may see construction on the ancestral tombs as an improper action."

I am going to eat them all. I mind-rant to Older One. If the heavens had any will, they would not have willed me to be a god.

Then thunder roars. Everyone is startled. So am I, but I do not show it.

But then the thunder gives me an idea. I turn to the court. "You are correct, counsel. We will speak to the heavens."

"You can do that, goddess?" One of the ministers says.

"Of course," Of course, anyone can talk to the heavens. It is not a lie—just look at the sky and yell.

"We have never heard of any of the gods being capable of such."

"We have the mandate from the heavens.

They sent a shooting star from the sky to appoint us. The land has chosen us. We are the god of Yanghe, so they will hear us." I start to pull lighting from the black clouds, to make it look like the heavens are behind me. "We will commence the ritual to communicate with the heavens in three days."

Lightning rolls and the sky booms. The ministers and their attendants squeal. I dart a quick look at Older One, hoping for an assurance that my power did not damage anything.

Older One simply looks amused.

Everyone is quiet and dazed, so I break the silence. "We are grateful that the great court of Yanghe will assist with the ritual."

"Of …of course, goddess," Minster Wa replies. "What shall we do?"

"Prepare a feast. We would want to give the heavens a proper welcome, wouldn't we?"

The heavens do not actually eat, so all the food will be given out to the poor afterward. I might as well feed the city while we're at it. And myself.

Everyone bows.

"Very well, let us get ready."

"The great and illustrious Yongdi! May you live a thousand years!" the hall says in unison.

The court makes their way out of the Long Hall. When they are gone and I am alone, Older One says, *You are getting clever, Young One.*

To think that I tried so hard to impress these folks. Fools and crybabies. We have to lie to soothe their little souls.

They're scared. We all get scared, Young One. You do too and so was I. And not everyone has the privilege and the power of the gods.

I huff. She pats me on the head. It is strangely soothing.

You summoned the first lightning, didn't you? I asked.

What do you mean?

You summoned the lightning to give me an idea.

You give me too much credit, Young One. The weather is the weather.

I don't believe it.

And what would the god who can clap a great thunder be scared of?

***

When I started living in the palace, I cried a lot. Nobody liked a girl who fished out of the river and lay in mud to sit on the throne. But the land had chosen and so they had to live with me, as I had to live with them.

So I spoke with politeness. I sat and slithered with poise. Even when being brushed and cleaned by servants, I cared not to lose the powder on my face and the pins in my hair. I learned to use chopsticks. I learned to read inked lines and letters, and then to write them. Many times, the ink from the brushes would smudge my dress.

The servants always kept silent and remained polite, but when I wanted tea, it was cold by the time I took the first sip. Many times, the meal was cleared before I could take my first bite. It was this that made me realize I preferred the Arowana the most out of the fish in the garden pond.

My eyes blurred with tears. I sat in my room, trying to read again the prophesied poem that started it all. How had I gotten here? Why had the heavens let me be here?

Earlier that day, I sat in the Long Hall being ignored by the court, like an idol. The ministers talked past me, thinking I knew nothing of taxes, trade, and harvests, even though Minister Yang and the tutors taught me about all sorts of subjects. Before daybreak and after nightfall, I studied everything from mathematics to poetic epics, agriculture to civic duty. I could recite the history of the empire from the time before the first dynasty until now, the fifth. But that did not matter. Even if I could discuss the entire Qon classic or multiply up to seven digits, they would still treat me as a stain on the tapestries.

The only people who came to see me were the desperate folk. They brought me their grievances—bandits in the outlying districts, sick children, bad weather, dry soil, flooding crops, or just plain poverty. And they left, still grieving. I could arrest the bandits, but as long as there were no jobs, they would be back or new ones would fill the empty spots. I could speed the recovery of the sick child, but they would get no better if they had no food. I could stop or summon the rain, but the streams would parch or flood somewhere else. Even the grandest city of the empire couldn't escape poverty and disaster. Even the greatest magic in the world couldn't go against the course of nature. And I barely understand either the magic or the world.

I clutched the leather scroll, looking at the squiggly characters.

The letter won't change from just staring at it, you know? You have to pick up the brush.

I scrambled and looked around. There should have been no one in my inner chamber, but I saw a large pair of eyes staring at me. I froze. A giant body filled the room. She had gray hair bunned under a crown. The endless black and olive tail stretched endlessly out of the maroon robe into the space beyond.

She smiled.

My tears had dried by then. I was no longer alone.

***

That was my first meeting with Older One. She has taught me many things. She taught me about the court and its politics, history and what has been carried on from the past. She also taught me magic and how it is perceived. I have learned that the real power is not to pull lightning, cure the sick, or swim in the sky. It is the magic to move the mind and the heart. This real magic is long and tedious.

I have molted and shed many times since then. I have grown longer.

So has the levee project.

"The great and venerated Yongdi, may you live a thousand years," says Duke Huan, a high-born noble with a long beard, long pointy ears, a long pair of feet, and an even longer lineage. "We all know how important the levee project is to you and the folks of Yanghe, but, Your Venerate, we do not have enough resources to keep this endeavor going. The farms are left untitled because all the workers are tending the levee, and the taxes for the project has been a burden to the belly."

The court nods in agreement.

Another sob story to keep workers working on their farms, I mind-whisper to Older One. *These nobles and riches.*

He does have a point, Young One.

His point is they want to keep their money and collect their crops and let everyone else deal with the expense of the levee which they will benefit from. They only send a minimal number of workers to work on the levee. They shift their wealth out of Yanghe so it does not look like they have extra gold to contribute to the project. They may be fools and crybabies, but they always find ways to keep their coin.

I turn my attention back to the court. They have planned this, planning to ambush me, most of them anyway. Minister Wa has been the one who sends the most folks and pays the most coin for the levee. He's now at the river directing his people. I, after all, made it look like the heavens gave him the most blessing during the ritual. "Duke Huan, you are right. It is our oversight to not consider the toll it would take on the citizens."

"I would not dare to say it was your oversight, your majesty. None of us has expected this."

Oh, look, I say to Older One, *I think I see a smirk on his face. He thinks he got me.*

Maybe you are being too hard on them.

You are not helping, Older One.

But Older One is not wrong. The duke has a point. At this rate, it would take decades to finish the project even if we can keep it going. However, I came prepared. I am aware of this issue and the duke's ambush.

Yanghe did not become grand from just sitting idle and showing off its gleams. Rice, jade, and timbers sail down the shining river. Spice, salt, and silk ride along the road that connects the far west to the far east. As the god and the troops guaranteed protection and security, the folk can trade, grow rich, and rest easy in this city. Far from conflict, cultures and knowledge gathered, exotic and rare merchandise flowed in. Craft-folks from many regions build shops and provide bespoke services. Scholars of many fields also come seeking knowledge or spreading it. The city entices folks to come, and so the gold flows. Yanghe may have its lacks but not in money.

And here is my counter, "So, we will sell the levee project," I announce.

The court gapes at me.

Oh, that is clever. So you knew what Duke Huan was trying to do? Older One says.

I have been keeping my ears to things.

I certainly have gotten soft. Perhaps the softness comes with age. She put her hand down on my head. *You will feel it someday, Young One.*

I will never be like you Older One. I always

have to spy and scheme to get what I need.
And have you spied and schemed?

* * *

The winter after the old god died—the one whose tomb was moved to make room for the levee—I snuck into the Vermilion Palace. I have never told anyone this tale, not even to Older One.

The marsh by the river was cold and harsh, so I usually slept on the street during those nights, but the city was being patrolled and cleaned as the entire Yanghe observed the mourning period for the god. The official announced that the god had passed because he had exhausted all his power to stop the raging flood. The citizens and many foreign visitors wore white, black, or blue. Incensed burned, candles were lit. The god was said to be both brave and kind. However, it seemed that kindness toward folks like me had died along with him.

By chance, ten noons before the mourning, a secret of the red palace passed by me while I fished in the depths of the wintry river. A small boat caught my eyes, being paddled against the

49

stiff wind. It looked too ordinary, as if it was artifice to mimic banality. But boats rarely fought the wind to get to where they were going.

Then a gentle voice spoke from the boat. "Blindfold the muted servants, take them to the passage under the Evening Water Hall. Have them make repairs to ensure the tunnel is well-maintained and safe. Then go alone to check the opening to the marsh. It has been a while since the passage has been cleaned. It's important that we have access to the dock in case of an unforeseen event. It is a tumultuous time now that the throne has been emptied."

Then after, I spent several suns and moons watching the marsh by the palace. Then, on the fourth day, in the fog of dawn, a lone servant came out from beneath the mud and grasses. I watched him disappear, then I went to the spot and found a well-hidden tunnel that led into the palace.

There were fewer guards in the inner palace now that the god no longer lived there. So I settled into the dark gap between buildings, where I would not be noticed, and tried to sleep. But the cold bit me, even there. The night wind picked up and wrapped itself around the structure like a viper. I woke up dazed. I staggered away, looking for warmth, when I noticed a window, slightly ajar. I clambered into the chamber, where I found a bed. Without enough energy to think, I slipped under the blanket and coiled to sleep.

Clop clop clop—a sound hit my ears. I awoke and froze. Dawn had barely broken. The sound of hooves on a wooden floor came from the hallway outside the room, followed by a conversation.

"Minister, the meteor will strike at the dawn of the new year," a female voice outside said.

"Are we still going with the prophecy of a fire-hair serpent, my lady?" the owner of the hooves responded.

"Yes. The new god will enter during the springtime with the kalugas in tow."

"Catching the kalugas will not be an easy task."

"Becoming a god isn't easy."

"Will the folks believe it? Won't they claim it to be a trick of sorcery?"

"It is a trick of sorcery, but they will believe it. We will have them think that was sent from the heavens. Suggest to the courts that they find sorcerers and scholars to inspect the scroll. The power imbued in the scroll and ink will be traced back to the second dynasty. No one has the kind of power to pull that off, not even the late god nor those who came before. That should give weight to the legitimacy of the prophecy. And The leather of the scroll should be made from a feathered reptile that only exists in myth."

"The Pixiu, my lady?"

"Older than that, minister."

'Older than that . . . Do you mean—"

"I will see you soon."

"I'll be waiting, my lady."

The hooves' sound faded down the hall, and the silence filled back the space.

I sneaked out through the window that I came in. That's when the spying ended and the scheming began.

***

"What do you mean, venerated?" Duke Huan asks.

What I mean is I plan to solve multiple

problems at once. I may not be able to leave this land since my power resides within it. But I have moved among the common folks, in disguise, many times in the dark after dusk or before dawn, sometimes quietly swimming alongside a boat or under a pier, gathering news, tales, and complaints. I have heard of the limited capacity of the current ports. Many merchants have to dock in the nearby villages or towns hauling their merchandise to the markets by cart. It is inefficient.

Of course I don't explain this. Let them perceive me as the all-knowing and ever watching.

"We will parse out the sections of the land that the levee will be built on and sell them to the highest bidders. The winners will help us to build and maintain the levee on their land. In compensation, they will be allowed to own piers for a hundred years on that land. All the earnings from the pier will go directly to the owner of the lease. And they will not be subject to any fee or tax."

It would allow the owners to grow rich for the next hundred years. But a hundred years is not forever. By the time the city got the land back,

Yanghe would be even more busy and prosperous than it is now. The pier that was built would bring in much more coin after the lease was up.

"Help in the construction?" Duke Huan says.

"Yes, Master Huan. we will use my power to help with any construction—the piers, the levee, the worker houses, whatever is needed for good levees and piers." This would also let me make sure everything was solidly built. "The workers will get to borrow our power to speed up the project. We have already spoken to a few of the merchants, and they seem interested, especially those from the Great Western Empire."

That, as I expected, made him even more flustered. "Let's . . . discuss this, Venerated. This humble subject with all deference and respect thinks you may be . . . too hasty. The implication of having foreigners control the piers, the dispute between buyers—"

"You're right to be concerned, Master Huan. But we have thought these matters through. With the many ports and piers, the price will remain low for any sailors to dock. Yanghe will have more trade, more visitors, more cultures, and more knowledge. The world will become more open, more invested in the future. So let us lead on the path forward. All the land sections will be marked distinctly by our powers, as will the contracts. We will oversee any disputes that may arise. Any of those who with malicious intent will face us."

I stare at the duke in the dark of his eyes.

He bows. "As you will it, Venerated."

The matter is settled, and the ministers then bow themselves out of my presence.

Now I will have to bow to the god of Yanghe, Older One says.

Don't be silly, Older One. I am no god. I only use the information I spied on.

Just like I had heard the prophecy of the scroll. I had chosen red mud to rub into my hair, chosen the Kaluga in order to conform to the scroll's description. I had schemed to conform to the will of the heavens, which didn't come from the heavens at all.

As any gods should, says Older One.

***

Older One? I call her with my mind. I have

not seen her for a couple of weeks now. She has not been accompanying me to my duty as much.

I grew busy with the levee. Many merchants and foreign envoys lined up to bid when the auction was announced. But rather than giving the project to whoever paid the most, we selected the buyers who were most likely to comply with the regulations. We also selected a variety of different folks to lower the chance of cartelizing and monopolizing. And countrykin like to deal with each other. By having a diversity of pier owners, sailors had more options for where to dock and whom to deal with. Although two out of ten piers were still in the hands of those of the court to keep them satisfied. I also granted Minster Wa a pier without payment. The rest of the court pulled out the money faster than they had ever had before.

Earlier today, I went to inspect the levees and the piers, making sure the structures followed common standards and guidelines. I summoned wind and wave to batter the levees to see how they stood. Most of it held up quite well, and the owners of the few spots that had overtopped were now making sturdier repairs.

The project, too, has been progressing better than I had expected. The workers quickly took up the power I lent them. Many were natural at using the power hopping around the site, strengthening their muscles, or even using it to float logs and stones. The power also prevented injuries and healed wounds, allowing workers to work at full capacity. Now there is no limit to how much power I can lend, but I will have to find ways to limit the ill-intent used.

"Older One."

I reach out with my voice this time, only for it to echo in the empty hall. I have been searching for her for many days now. The garden, the kitchen, the Long Hall, the Evening Hall, even the secret passage where I had first entered the palace. Yet there is no sign of the giant goddess.

I return to my quarters. I sit at the desk full of neatly stacked papers, and stare at a sky that is as red as my mood.

How could she just leave? The levee just started, and I am getting busier and busier. Does she not think this is important? Does she not care about her city, her citizens, or . . . me?

I leave my desk to get fresh air. I slither out into the outer hallway, passing chambers and decorative trees and bushes.

But I knew the answers, didn't I? I just have been ignoring the truth. I had found my place, my counsel, my friend, and made myself instrumental in shaping the city's future. So I pretended that everything was right and fine.

But it was not. There was no heaven to send down a rock from the sky, just one very big mean god. The whole farce was to trick the court and the folk, but the trick was on me, too . . . I am nothing more than an instrument to do Older One's biddings.

My tail led me to the garden. As the sun settles into the horizon, I stare at the darkening pond, whose inhabitants now look much less appetizing, now that I am admitting the truth to myself.

Older One was the lady outside the hallway when I snuck into the palace. She and Minister Yang. It was he who let slip the secret about the passage when he passed by me on the boat. They set everything up for me to be here, in the palace, to be the god. Not happenstance, not the heavens. Because they knew.

They knew the river girl who lived alone out by the river was not really a river girl who lived out by the river.

**

"Captain, this is all the money I have for the kalugas. I will be sure to pay you the remainder one day," I said.

The scents of salt, spice, and tea swirled in the air of the captain's cabin. North, west, and south met here in the east. News, favor, and gold were exchanged here at the port of Yanghe, and I had been spying for them for years. Morally questionable, but any trader worth their salt would have ways to fetch any tales before they became widely known. A farm burn down meant buying all the grain before the price hike. A war about to start meant buying all the wood for the coffins. Who bought what or who traded with who drove the market. I may as well be part of that.

"No need, kid," the crow-folk captain said. His black wings protruded out of his Great Western Empire-style silk shirt. He was seated behind a writing table, his left wooden leg stretched, relaxed. "You've been good sailing with us, and you helped us beat the Blue Guild with your listening." His left fore-talon handed back the money purse. His other fore-talon took lit rolled paper out of his beak and exhaled smoke. "But are you sure you want to do this?"

"Captain, there's very little risk. I've escaped many situations, and I know the secret way in and out of the palace. I'll be fine."

"I know, kid. I'm not worried about your plan failing. I'm worried about it succeeding. You won't be able to leave Yanghe when you become its god, you know? You can keep sailing with us. Isn't that why you asked me to take you from your home village? To see the wider world? You have the brain for trade and picking up information."

I'd looked down at the deck's floor. I knew I wanted to do this but couldn't explain why, even to myself. "Yes, captain, I love sailing and trading with you, the crew, and this boat. I love having an upper hand over the Blue Guild or the Lotus, the teasing of information, the competition, the negotiation. But I didn't get myself into and then kicked out of the imperial school because I simply wanted to learn things or make money. There's . . . something there in the palace. Something beyond this world. I need to be there"

"All right, kid, if that's what you really want. I guess one can't stop one's fate."

"It's not merchant-like to hang plans on fate, captain. We take the opportunities where we can and when we can."

The captain smirked. "Here's the other stuff you requested."

"Thank you, Captain. You've taught me a lot in the past years, and I'm looking forward to working with you, though in a different manner."

The crow captain nod.

But before I left, I turned.

"Captain, how did you know about the boat paddling out in the wind in the middle of the winter?"

The captain could only smile and said, "a whisper from an old friend, kid."

Afterward, I dipped my hair in Ashwood, red clay, and henna—not just red mud—to conform to the prophecy. And as I'd pretended for the last few months, I would tell everyone, including myself, that I was just a girl who lived by the river and knew nothing more than the river and its fish.

***

The red sky is turning deep blue and pink-purple. The moon shines its pearly light. The shadow deepens and lengthens.

That was why she picked me didn't she? To do her spying and scheming? Now I am here all alone, trapped in the palace. I should have heeded the captain's words. The heavens and the ghosts of my predecessors are punishing me for disrespecting them.

The sun is now almost gone from the sky and the lanterns' light casts large shadows. The darkness makes the palace feel immensely vast. I feel small, like a pawn, like when I was treated as an idol in the court.

Is that all you really are? Is that all you're going to admit?

I spin around looking for the speaker of the voice, but there is only empty air. I turn left and right, but there is on one. Then I see a shadow of an endless serpent's tail stretches in front of me. I trace it, hoping to see its owner. My eyes stop back at the dark pond.

I stand staring at the older god. Except that

she looks young now, youthful and small. Her hair is loose, and she wears an evening gown. She looks straight at me . . . gazing.

Gazing out of the reflection in the dark water lit by the lantern's light like a mirror . . .

And it is only then that I finally realize. I realize all the lies, all the layers of pretending. I have convinced myself and everyone else that I was nothing more than a river girl turned accidental goddess, telling myself that I had never seen the sea, pretending that the red clay on my hair was a bumbling clumsiness. So I could really be the mud girl, the clueless. Because everyone looks down on the incompetent, the non-threat, they become unguarded. If the rich and the noble had sensed a hint of my scheme, my real competence, they would have used everything against me before I was ready, before I could figure out who was the ally, who was the enemy and their scheme.

But I also let myself think that I was just the merchant's spy. A girl with a bit of ambition. I pretended to be the god of old to my younger self. If I had let myself take the throne knowing I was the rightful god and not a common folk, I would have simply solved everything with the sorcery and authority of the god. I would not have mastered the story and beliefs of the people.

The story and belief are not only for others but also for me.

I now understand who I am. I understand the true power I inherit, the power that extends beliefs and legends. I can now see the invisible chaotic, and twisted rivers, touch it, swim in it. I feel my own death and what comes afterwards. I feel my own birth and the time before. I feel all of me that branches into many different worlds. I feel all of me that I could learn from, all of me that would help fulfill my duty. I feel me across all of worlds and those in parallels.

I feel all of times.

I am here not by some outside destiny, using me as a pawn. I am here by right. Here is my place. I am here to shape the court, the city, and the world into its rightful path.

My path.

I remember what I must do. I head back to my room. I grind the ink stone and put my brush to the parchment. I ink what needed to be done for the time long past, for the time before the first dynasty. I write that wood generated fire but overcame earth, earth generated metal but overcame water, and so on. The prophesies, the principles on which the city will be built.

It seems that to be a god is to be a liar, even lying to oneself.

I smile.

***

I have gotten used to swimming through the chaotic torrent of time. I arrive at the bank of the swelling Golden River. The rain pours from the wrathful night sky. Looking across the water, I see the grand city and its god. He is controlling the river with his given power. He is the same kinfolk as Minister Yang — goat, ox, and tiger features, with talons for hands, strong yet gentle. I feel sorrow for what I am about to do.

The sky flashes its anger. The river rushes its torrent. The god is wet and exhausted, preventing the relentless water from flooding the city. Rain and wind hurl hard. All the citizens are sheltering in place. Only gods can withstand this violence.

I remain dry.

I reach for the power of the land of this time. It responds. Then I feel through the power, my power. I feel all the land, my land. I feel all the livings and the things that reside on this ground and sky. I feel the warmth of the god of this time. He is warm and soft like a lantern lighting, the path in the cold and the dark. I hold his power. The power that is struggling against the raging river.

Then I grasp that warm glow. I breathe sorrowfully and take back what I have given him and all those who came before him.

Between the water and the city, the lone body falls, carried away by the rain and the river. He was brave, kind, and good. That's why I picked him and why I picked all the gods of Yanghe. I bow toward his remains for fulfilling his duty, the duty that is now mine.

I calm the Golden River. The torrent subsides. The rain slows. I look toward the night sky.

Soon spring will come, I need to get ready for Young One.

And it's about time I write about the heavens.

The Ace of Rules

S. L. Johnson

The holding cell is well-used, but clean. Made for the native Tyulti population rather than the Earth-born, everything is wrong-sized for the group of human women that have arrived over the last few hours. Linda closes her eyes for a moment. Her stomach cramps again. The feeling subsides, and she checks out the cell. Most of the other five women are silent, but their sideways glances speak of suspicion and fear.

Linda guesses them to be a range of nationalities and languages. Two older German speakers occupy the lone, sheetless bunk bed and hold a rapid-fire conversation in low voices. Before she can reach any conclusions about the others, she feels tears welling up. She closes her eyes again and forces herself to think of something else. She calculates whether her worst student has any chance of passing her English class. Maybe. The tears subside.

Linda wishes she had stayed on Earth. She'd swap this cell for an Earth police station cell. Or even a hospital. At least then she'd know why she was here.

The dingy passageway is muted now. Earlier, a constant stream of Tyulti enforcers passed through on their way to other holding cells. The stream became a dribble, then a drip, then no one for a long time. Hours passed. How many? She replays the last few days from memory as she waits.

**

"Earth-born people play games to learn how to obey rules." Linda pursed her lips, red pen wavering over the homework assignment she was grading but moved on. "Sokker is a good game for learning rules." This time a circle. "Earth-born people learn when to bent rules," at this Linda's pen darted in to change the 't' into a 'd,' "by the use of fowls." Another mark.

A knock on her apartment door startled her. Who could it be so long after sunset? Sitting at her dining table grading essays on her students' favorite Earth sports, the knock could have been a relief. It could have been her neighbor, or even the building manager, but it wasn't.

The monitor attached to the door frame illuminated as she approached, and Linda sucked in a tense breath: three Tyulti in Enforcement garb. Near-human except for coats of fur that blended into the gray-black of their uniforms, two of them stood at relative ease with rifle-sized diasho cradled in their arms. The shortest one, still much taller than Linda, was empty-handed.

She considered ignoring the visitors. But Steve Masser had ignored a visit from the enforcers last year. Mr. Enio, the Tyulti who had recruited them all from Earth, had told the teachers that he'd been repatriated because of a family emergency. No one had ever heard from him again.

Linda opened the door.

"Aaahhhhh," said the tallest, best-groomed member of the group. "Hello, you speak Tyult?" He blinked. Linda also blinked politely, failing to read the situation.

"No, sorry. Can I help you?"

The official spoke in short, Tyult syllables to both of his junior staff, who answered in the negative with regretful head tilts.

"Passport? Passport? See?" the officer asked with a smile.

"Oh, sure", Linda said, holding up her first finger. "Wait one minute, please."

The officer nodded. "One minute, yes."

Linda grabbed her Earth passport, bringing it back to the door.

After inspecting the document page by page, the officer asked, "Visa? University Visa?"

Linda frowned. "It's in process; I don't have it yet."

The officer at the door asked again, with bared teeth—a Tyult frown.

Linda held up her finger again. She scrambled to grab her handheld, a thin plastic oblong that lit up as she lifted it from the tabletop. Returning to the door, she pulled up the contact details for Mr. Enio, the recruiter of all alien faculty.

"Ahh," the Enforcer said with relief. With a sharp word, one of the younger males produced a smaller handheld. The young officer tapped it against Linda's device, the diasho dangling in his other hand.

"Thank you, that is all," the officer said, and the trio strode back to the apartment building's elevator while Linda looked at their retreating forms, perplexed.

She closed the door and leaned against it, only then noticing the sweat rolling down her back. She texted Mr. Enio, "Hi. Enforcers came to my home asking about visa status, please advise?"

Wracking her brain, Linda tried to remember what Steve had said in his last appearances in the teacher's room. Something about regulations? Interpretations of what's true? As hard as she tried, she couldn't quite remember. Steve complained a lot.

No reply from Mr. Enio. She sat back down to her students' assignments but couldn't focus. At midnight, she went to bed, spending the night with restless dreams.

The Next Day

"Did you get the fuzzbutts at your door?" Ron asked, his Spanish accent nearly unnoticeable. All the Earth-born instructors were around the long, trestle-style table occupying the middle of the Teacher's Room. A couple of Tyult professors, their fur variegated with patches of silver hair suggesting age, were at smaller desks on the sides of the room pecking at computers, creating student worksheets in various Earth languages.

"Shhhh! Don't say fuzzbutts. You can't say that," Linda said.

"Why not," Ron said, "Clement does." Down the table, one of the Mandarin professors sat, reading a book. He turned his head at the mention of his name and grinned.

"Clement is not a nice person," said Raia, just above a whisper.

"I'm *right here*," Clement didn't turn from his book as he spoke.

The group fell silent.

"So? You all had visitors too?" Ron sat back, stretching in his chair.

Clement looked at Ron and rolled his eyes before speaking again, this time directed at a female Tyult on a computer facing the wall opposite him. "Ms. Chirgaa, we all had enforcers visit us last night to check our papers; do you think we're in trouble?"

Ms. Chirgaa twisted around, considering us with an unreadable expression. "*Phe skagaan Tyulti.*"

Everyone knew what this meant. *This is Tyulti.*

Ms. Chirgaa narrowed her eyes. "Did you remember to blink?"

Everyone blinked in reply.

"Are you all carrying your Earth passports

more importantly? You must always obey the laws here." The deep voice from the far side of the office surprised everyone, including Ms. Chirgaa. Professor Emeritus Katkop was a mountain of well-groomed fur and manners, but he rarely engaged in conversation with the rest of the department. We stopped blinking, and we shifted in our chairs without speaking.

"Not so good," Professor Katkop said.

***

Footsteps and muffled Tyult voices approach. Linda looks up. A giant, dark-furred, enforcer approaches the cell with Raia, a Bulgarian teacher from Linda's university. The enforcer opens the cell door and pushes Raia into the space. The women in the cell slink away from the guards. Linda raises a hand, catching Raia's attention, and, with a quick nod of greeting, her friend moves to Linda's side. The shadow-colored enforcer stands near the open cell door, waiting as a pair of smaller male Tyults push a hovering grav cart laden with small blocks wrapped in something white in front of the open cell door. Next to the stack are a silver thermos and paper cups.

The furred duo positions the cart across the entrance, and the taller enforcer gestures at Linda and another woman.

Dismayed at being singled out, Linda feels her stomach tighten again. One of the furred guards taps, impatient, on the metal thermos, and, as if in response, her stomach growls. She and the other prisoner step up and blink several times. The guards give one cursory blink in return and the taller Tyult oversees them as they dole out food and drink to their cellmates.

Linda conceals a shudder as she passes Raia a cup of lukewarm tea with a sandwich wrapped in what feels like toilet paper.

"Are you okay?" she mutters as Raia takes the food. The sound of people chewing, and the muted conversation of the German women continue in the background.

"Yeah, I'm fine. You?"

Linda tries on a brief smile as they unwrap their sandwiches. The bitter stink of local tea permeates the cell. Raia sets the cup on the ground, untasted, and takes a bite of her sandwich. Not really a sandwich—a thick salty protein paste between two layers of spongy vegetable slices—but both of them devour their portions.

Raia wipes her mouth with the paper wrapper and asks, "Has anyone questioned you yet?"

Linda swallows the last bite of her sandwich. "No, what do you mean? Like, they took you somewhere and asked you questions about—I don't even know—what did they ask?"

"It all seemed pointless." She brushes crumbs into the sandwich wrapper. "But if they haven't formally arrested us, that means they want something. Answers."

"They can't round us up like animals, put us in a pen, and ask us questions."

"You think you have the same rights here as on Earth," Raia says. "That's very naïve of you."

Linda spends the next half hour thinking about Raia's words and listening to her cellmates complain softly in German. Eventually, Linda notices the rhythm of the German ladies' speech changing. She watches them laying cards on the bare mattress. Raia and one of the other cellmates watch over their shoulders. Linda can't recognize the game they're playing, but drifts over and joins Raia behind a woman whose white hair is pulled into an untidy ponytail.

The ponytailed player cranes her neck around to look at Linda with glittering eyes. "You know why they don't play games on Tyult?" she says. "They don't play games here because they don't understand bluffing, and they don't do well with ambiguity. Here, everything is all rules." She stares at her hand and places a card on top of the small pile between the players.

Her opponent, younger, but still mature in age, checks the card on the mattress, then her own hand. Her face drops as she lays her own hand down in defeat.

The older woman turns to Linda again.

"You can bend the rules here, but in parameters that make little sense to Earth-borns. And bluffing? We Earth-born use it to win back home, but perhaps here not so much. We still don't understand the rules of the game on Tyult do we?"

The sound of the rusty lock on the cell door interrupts the German. A female Tyulti officer, her somber uniform accented by her deer-brown fur, peers at the prisoners from outside the cage.

"Linda Nash?" The guard says.

Linda raises her hand. The officer issues orders in tumbling syllables of Tyult while motioning for Linda to exit the cage. After a short walk, her escort deposits her in a small windowless room with a metal table and two chairs, all bolted to the floor. The door is closed and locked behind her. Linda surveys the room then sits down in the cold metal chair facing the door. The seat warms underneath her as she waits. She waits and waits. She shifts in the chair as parts of her rear end go numb. Has she been forgotten? She considers getting up to bang on the door, then it swings open. A dignified Tyult female with dark, lush fur, enters and greets Linda in near-unaccented English.

"I'm very sorry to have displaced your day, Miss Linda." Displaced? "Let's try to get you released sooner rather than later, heh? I am Captain Roxgra, and I am here to sort things out." As she sits across the table from Linda, she smooths her perfectly tidy uniform jacket.

Maybe this wouldn't be so bad after all—but why lock everyone up to begin with? Linda remembers to use her courteous blinks. The captain gives one blink in reply.

"This is more than an administrative mistake, or an inconvenience—" Linda says, but the captain grimaces and she falters.

"Some disturbing intelligence has come to light over the course of the last few days. The Ministry of the Interior is determined to find out if there is a threat to the Tyulti Republic. Unfortunately, the rumor suggests the involvement of foreign educators in private universities. We have to determine the truth of this intelligence."

Linda scrambles to recall anything about political instability and university educators but draws a blank.

"So... your most logical response was to detain all Earth-borns who teach? All of us?" Unbelievable.

"Yes, of course, let's get right to the point: have you heard anything that might apply to our investigations?"

Linda bites off a sarcastic reply and stops to consider the captain's question.

"No, not at all. University adjuncts are not really people with agendas. We're simple people who want to make a living and see the galaxy."

"Sure, sure," says Captain Roxgra. "How

about your work permit? Why don't you have one?"

Linda wrinkles her eyebrows. "Mr. Enio from personnel told me that's a visa processing issue. The Enforcement Bureau manages work and residence permits. My papers have been in process for months; I wouldn't mind if you looked into that for me."

"Why are you working without a permit?"

Linda's heart begins pounding. Has the school screwed this up?

"Because that's how I was told it's done." She wipes her palms on her trousers.

"You know you could be prosecuted for working without a permit,"

What? Is this Tyulti trying to game me into working for her as an informant? Maybe that German woman didn't know what she was talking about.

"What about the school?" Linda said.

"Of course, the school could be fined as well, but you should have gone back to your planet of origin to wait for your visa approval to come through."

Linda feels her blood pressure, the pressure in her entire body, seeking release. It's hard to keep from shouting, so she speaks with deliberate slowness. "Every single language teacher I have met here has done the same thing that I have. Are you suggesting that you are going to arrest every Earth-born teacher on the planet and jail them when it's your higher education system that is at fault?"

The captain remains silent for a moment and as Linda's body unclenches, Captain Roxgra says, "Remind me why you have chosen to work without a work permit again?"

"They said this is how everyone does it. Everyone I've met is doing the same thing. '*Phe skagaan Tyulti*,' even I know that one, 'This is Tyulti.'"

"It seems to me that you have misplaced your trust," Roxgra says. "You are innocently working for an institution that may have intentions that are less than honest."

"And what about the other people you've locked up?" says Linda, gesturing over her shoulder.

"Don't worry about them. Worry about you." Captain Roxgra pulls a business card from her breast pocket, along with Linda's passport. "Let's see how we can fix everything. I'll hold on to this." She waves the passport, then slides it back into her pocket. With her other hand, she passes over the business card. "And you can hold on to this."

Linda takes the card with both hands, staring at it as if it's just introduced itself.

"Let's arrange a chat every Tenth Day afternoon, shall we?" Roxgra says. "Once you are done with work. Go home, relax for an hour. After that—call me. I'd like to know more about the opinions of the faculty in your department. In particular, I'd like to know if they express any political sentiments, on or off duty. I want to know what kind of phone conversations you overhear them having, and who comes to visit them. Listen to the students, and what they say about their teachers. Do you have questions?"

"Yes, at least fifty," Linda says. Captain Roxgra gives her a sharp look and pats the passport in her pocket. "What about my fellow Earth colleagues? Will they be reporting on me? What about Tyulti staff?"

"Don't worry about your colleagues, worry about you. I suggest you start paying attention. I'll be happy to hear about emotions, expressions, body language, anything you can share until you learn more. Effort means a lot to me."

"What about Raia? She's—" The captain holds up a hand, and Linda stops speaking.

"Good evening, Linda. Don't worry, I'll be watching you." The captain stands and knocks on the door.

Another uniformed Tyult deposits Linda outside the main gates of the Civil Enforcement Offices. It's the middle of the night. A self-driving *emyst* beeps in the whirling traffic, and Linda raises her hand to flag it down. It stops dead and reverses in her direction. Other cars veer around it, honking. Linda's trembling slows as she gets in and directs the vehicle to take her home.

Despite the sunny, clear weather, Linda stays inside all weekend. The hours of the day melt into irrelevance. Everything is unreal, unreliable, including the sun in the sky. She paces. She stops. She sits and stares. Several times she reaches for her handheld to call her fellow teachers, Ron, or Raia, then sets it back down. None of her colleagues reach out to her.

I'm an alienated alien trapped on an alien world, Linda thinks, but she can't bring herself to laugh. She can't grade papers or write lesson plans. She doesn't book the trip with Ron that she'd been planning for the midterm holiday to the Irium waterfalls. She exists paralyzed, pinned down like a moth on a board, under a Tyult gaze.

Monday morning, when she arrives at the teacher's room, most of her colleagues are bent over laptops or papers, oblivious to her arrival. Raia isn't there. Linda drops her briefcase on the conference table in the middle of the room with a thud. The other faculty raise their heads, but then return their gazes to their paper and computers.

"So," Linda asks, elongating the "o" with a casualness that is anything but casual. "What did everyone get up to Friday night?"

Ron looks at her with a pained expression but says nothing. Everyone else ignores her. The discomfort in Ron's reaction makes Linda chest clench. Something breaks inside her.

"Where's Raia?"

"She was here, but she left an hour ago," says Ron. "She left with Clement."

"Right," Linda says to the air. She seats herself at a battered communal wall tablet, taps a stylus on the screen, and waits for it to complete its start sequence. Once the tablet comes to life, she types in a search for the address of the Earth consulate, copies it onto a sheet of scratch paper, repacks her belongings, and leaves. In her peripheral vision, she catches a few of her former colleagues lifting their heads to watch her departure.

An *emyst* drops her off in a neighborhood of suburban apartments with paint peeling from jumbled boxes cluttered with pastel-colored balconies. The consulate itself is a large cement bunker, several stories tall, surrounded by an imposing wall. Along the wall, a disorganized line of Tyulti hold papers. The line moves in fits and starts; each group takes anxious steps toward the gate. On the other side of the road, a series of office supply shops offering passport-style photos are interspersed with seedy-looking peppermilk houses with open fronts. The vendors of the traditional hot, spicy Tyult beverage are swamped with people watching the line from crowded wooden tables. Some of the customers juggle glasses of peppermilk and their papers. Two Tyulti take photos of the people in the queue from their seats, and a few ignore the show, tapping on their handhelds.

Linda ignores the line and strides up to the Tyulti enforcers at the gate. She ignores a low muttering from the people at the front of the line.

"Appointment paper?" asks an official in heavily-accented English.

"No, no, I'm an Earth citizen," Linda says. "I need to speak to someone immediately."

"No appointment, no enter," says the official and he turns back to the line to reach for a young Tyulti woman's extended papers.

"No, no, it's an emergency."

The Enforcer pauses with his hands full of documents and squints at Linda. "Passport?"
"I don't have it. I have my driver's license, birth certificate, and social security card."

The police officer moves all the paper into his right hand and extracts a slip of paper from a plastic sleeve nailed to the concrete wall next to him. "Call number for emergency appointment."

Linda plucks the paper from his hands. She strides across the street to the nearest, busiest peppermilk shop and raises her voice. "Does anyone speak English? I'll pay 100 refedi to use someone's handheld for a few minutes."

A young female with long fur responds. "Please use mine. You don't need to give me any money."

Linda thanks her and takes the device, which is in English. She moves to a corner of the cafe, covering the receiver and her mouth with her hand as it rings through. She looks around, unsure if any of the Tyulti watching the line have turned their attention to her.

"Hello, hello? Oh, hi, look I need help. I am outside the consulate now. Something terrible has happened, and—no, no. I have literally walked away from my whole life. I was detained by the Enforcers, something about political unrest. I need to see someone. No, I don't have access to the Network right now. I am across the road from you at one of the peppermilk vendors. Can someone come out and get me? I swear to God, just help me please. It really is an emergency. Hasn't anyone else shown up like this? Ok—ok—yes. Alright, my name is Linda Nash. Yes, N-A-S-H. I can be there in 30 seconds. Oh, ok, I'll wait a minute then. Ok, thank you, goodbye." Linda pushes the disconnect button on the handheld, handing it back to its owner with a strained but grateful smile. "Thank you."

"*Upgo ke* I was able to help you," the young woman replies.

"Thank you…. Are you sure I can't give you some money in return?"

The stranger smiles. "No. Perhaps we will encounter each other on Earth one day. If we do, you can buy me a drink. Now, if you will excuse me, it is almost my appointment time."

"Good luck."

They step out of the café together into the gray, watery light of the street. The Tyulti woman veers right to join the queue, while Linda crosses the street toward the entrance to the consulate.

The sentry's handheld bursts into static laden Tyulti as she gets closer. After a brief conversation, he meets her gaze and says,

"Name?"

"Linda Nash."

The officer grunts and gestures her into the secure area inside the gate. Linda passes through several stages of security, fields questions about the purpose of her visit, then enters the body scanner. She deposits her belongings, except for her wallet and papers, into a locker, and receives a key with stern instructions not to lose it. Her wallet and papers are hand-inspected before being run through another scanning machine. Afterwards, the Tyult security officers herd her and a cluster of strangers into an elevator. A human United Nations marine escorts them up one floor and guides them along a breezeway to the consulate fifty meters away. At the entrance, the visitors produce their documents for another Marine, and again explain their purpose for visiting. A brunette Earth-born woman in a gray pantsuit meets Linda.

"Are you Linda Nash?"

Linda nods.

"Please come with me."

The official turns down a corridor to the left., then opens the last door to lead her through a busy office into a glass cubicle with the blinds drawn shut. A sandy-haired Earth-born man in his early forties rises from behind his desk.

"John Scanlon, nice to meet you."

"Linda Nash, thanks for seeing me so quickly."

After a firm handshake with no blinking, they

settle into two guest chairs.

"Linda, I think we already have an idea what's happened and why you are here, but would you mind telling me your entire story? Would it be alright if I recorded it?"

"Sure." Linda explains the events of the last few days.

"Well, I should tell you first off that you're the third person today that has shown up under the same circumstances." He taps his fingers on his knee. "I'm required to ask what you want from us."

"I want out. I want to go home. I don't know what's going on." She waves her hands in front of her. "And I don't want to find out." John nods. "I didn't sign up for this; I just came here for the job and to see the galaxy. Can you get me out of here?"

"Let me explain how this works. When an Earth-born has a personal emergency, we can arrange an emergency travel document. It will get you through immigration formalities so you can get back home. We can even get you on a flight home if you need it. However, you'll have to repay the costs to the United Nations, and you won't be able to get a new passport or leave

Earth again until you repay those expenses."

"Not a problem."

John raises a hand. "The issue that's less routine is that this is a fairly unstable political situation. We aren't sure what's happening, and getting you to the spaceport itself, as well as through passport control, may be an issue. Residents of this world need an exit permit to leave, and you won't have one. You'll be depending on the good grace of the border agent to let you out. Sometimes it happens and sometimes it doesn't."

Linda breathes deep. "What if I had a family emergency?"

"A government representative would never tell you to claim something like this, but I can see that this would be an easy answer. People use it. Sometimes it works, sometimes it doesn't. The Tyult people are sticklers for the rules, although our culture is so messy to them that sometimes they make allowances for us. You'd have to take your chances. Are you still game?" John's face is neutral, but his head is bobbing slightly, as if his subconscious is telling Linda to take this chance.

"Get me out of here. Please. As soon I as

possibly can."

"It's going to take a few hours to sort out your travel document and draw up the promissory letter for you to sign. I suggest you stay here on the consulate grounds until everything is ready. If you're okay with that, I'll ask you to leave your proof of identity with me. I'll set you up in a room with the other folks that have made it in here. How's that?"

"Yes, this sounds great."

John takes the papers she holds out. "We're hoping that the left hand doesn't know what the right hand is doing. With luck. you'll be able to waltz right out."

"*Phe skagaan Tyulti.* This is Tyulti, as they keep telling me here."

"Exactly, and what it really means is that we'll never quite understand what's going on."

John leads Linda out of his office into another glassed area with blinds, a long meeting table, and uncomfortable looking chairs holding two other Earth-born. Linda is surprised to find Raia and Clement looking back at her. Relief seeps into her chest.

"Well look who else made it," Raia says. "Would you like something to drink? They said we could help ourselves."

Linda dashes around the table and embraces her colleague. Some of the tension melts out of her shoulders. Raia rolls her eyes, but pats Linda on the shoulder in return.

"Drink?"

"Uh, maybe later?" says Linda, nonplussed.

Linda raises a hand to greet Clement and he nods in reply.

"What happened to you, Linda?" he says. "When you didn't come in to work, I thought the Tyultis kept you in custody."

"I was late, I haven't slept all weekend. I thought—I assumed—" Linda tries to stop tears from welling up. She sniffs. "You heard about Steve last year, right?"

"I heard he had a family emergency. He didn't even say goodbye," Clement says.

"Aha," Raia says. "The old family emergency excuse. I heard someone bluffed their way out of their job contract last year by having a family emergency so she wouldn't get stuck paying penalties for breaking the contract."

"I always wondered why no one stays more than a year or two," says Clement. "They wanted me to become an informer, and they took my passport. I had to agree at the time, but I spoke to Raia in the office this morning and we decided to come here."

"And you trust Clement?" Linda said to Raia.

"I'm *right here*," says Clement, with a ghost of a smile.

Raia shrugs. "That's what you get for not learning to blink; you're *labeled*."

"Yeah, yeah, bad expat, whatever."

"What happened to *you*?" Linda asks Clement.

He grins at her question. "They didn't have my name spelled right in their records, so they couldn't hold me. Those are the rules. I was probably back home before you even arrived."

"Well done, Clement," Raia says. "You're a quick thinker."

"Not so much that. The same thing happened to me back on Earth in Lanzhou."

"This has happened to you before?" Linda asks.

"Less fur, same issues." Clement shrugs.

"I'm surprised to see you here, Linda," Raia says. "Either you're braver than I thought, or you're here as a spy." The bottom falls out of Linda's stomach.

Raia laughs. "You should see your face. Calm down, I'm just kidding."

Clement chuckles.

"I'm looking forward to getting off Tyult," Raia says. "How about you guys?"

"Definitely. Do you two understand what's happening?"

"Look, paranoia against us aliens is par for the course," Clement says. "I'm not sure why teachers keep getting brought in when they don't really want us on this planet."

The door to the meeting room opens and Mr. Scanlon steps in, holding several sheaves of papers. He passes each packet out.

"We've hired an emyst with a Tyulti driver for the three of you. We've paid him cash in advance to take you to Off-world Departures at the spaceport." Linda shuffles through the stack of documents as he continues speaking. "This is what we can offer for now, without really having a full understanding of what is going on with the Tyulti government. Thanks for your patience, I wish you all the best on your way home."

Linda and her companions return their locker keys downstairs at security to collect their belongings. Linda keeps swallowing in an attempt to control the nausea that's been slowly rising from her gut. A Tyult staff member escorts them to the emyst waiting at a side gate, labeled "STAFF EXIT." The gate rumbles open and deposits Linda, Raia, and Clement on the sidewalk, where a grumpy driver with patchy fur waits for them. Raia jumps in the front, while Clement and Linda slide into the back seats. Linda cracks her window a fraction, trying to breathe. She didn't know she could feel panic at the same time as relief.

Almost there, almost there, she repeats to herself all the way to the airport. In the stack of papers on her lap is the thin booklet serving as her emergency passport and her original identity documents. Tucked inside the travel document is a printout for the next Earth departure—a ticket to Beijing, departing four hours later. Linda jams all the papers into her satchel. Her fingers tremble with nothing to hold on to.

At the Spaceport, the check-in procedure is a noisy blur. A buzzing fills her ears. She imitates Clement and Raia going through the document checks. Nausea surges as she receives a boarding pass from the customer service agent. Clenching her teeth and breathing in through her nose, she approaches a sign with an arrow showing in Tyulti script and several other languages "PASSPORT CONTROL." Clement and Raia stop next to her. They exchange worried glances.

It's going to be fine. I can do this. We'll all be fine. We wouldn't have gotten this far if it weren't fine.

The nausea fades, and Linda takes one step forward.

"Let me go first," she says. "If anything goes wrong, pretend you need the toilet or something." Raia gestures her ahead with a flourish. Linda joins the line ahead of them, ignoring the stomach cramps which have returned like a punch to her gut.

Let me be done with this, let me be done with this, let me be done with this.

With her emergency passport and boarding pass in hand, she approaches the next empty booth and sets her documents on the counter. She draws in a breath, prepared to spin a story about her sister, her only surviving relative, in hospital, alone, and penniless.

She catches a movement out of the corner of her eye. Someone is at her left shoulder. It's Captain Roxgra. Linda's breath catches. The captain moves around the kiosk to stand next to the agent, speaking to her in Tyulti. The woman replies while entering a series of keystrokes on her terminal. Linda's hope fades, and she wonders what will happen if she vomits on a government official.

"Don't worry," the captain says and meets Linda's eyes without blinking. "I told her to grant you an exit visa under my authority. Of course, we don't want trouble with the Earth authorities. Very clever of you to bend the rules with new documents." She picks up the thin booklet and waves it at Linda, then sets it back in front of the agent, who continues typing. "This is the second-best solution for us—if you foreigners leave and don't come back. Please remember—" Captain Roxgra pauses. "Don't. Come. Back." She pulls Linda's open passport in front of her and, removing a pen from a utility pocket on her shoulder, she scribbles on one of the pages before handing it back to the passport official, who examines the markings, then stamps them. The thunk vibrates down in the pit of nausea, but a kernel of hope soothes Linda's stomach.

The agent slides Linda's documents back across the ledge, and Linda picks them up.

"Have a pleasant flight," Captain Roxgra says. The officer crosses to the next booth, where Raia stands, and Linda sees Raia freeze with her mouth open as Roxgra speaks quietly. Linda glances at Clement, in line behind Raia, then back at the open passage to the airside section of the spaceport.

Linda takes one last deep breath as she passes through the lane to the space-side of the terminal. It takes her some time to walk to her destination at the end of the terminal and she checks her boarding pass. She is hours early, the first passenger to arrive at gate eighteen under the sign reading "Earth: Beijing."

She opens her passport with trembling hands. Still alone at the gate, there are no witnesses. The Earth consulate would never know if she disappeared here. Was that what happened to Steve?

She doesn't notice the airport security officers approaching as she leafs through the pages. It's only when she is thrown down on the floor and cuffed, her face inches from the single stamped page, that she can read the captain's note. Underneath her exit stamp, she discerns the following words, written in English:

"I was bluffing."

The Fourth of Tranquility

M.C.S. Levine

Reverberating through the ground (the air here barely carries sound), thumping drums herald the beginning of Remembrance Day on Tranquility. Each year on the fourth of Chetyud, wing-gliders cease their workaday commutes. Freed to fly the indigo skies, they ride the thermals, swirling up and down from the heights of the tallest towers out to the limits of the Area, their pilots sheathed in glittering foil biosuits reserved for the most exuberant of festivals.

We gather in the golden-pink-windowed Central Zome, all of us New Children, our scribs alight with strange images of Terra, the Last Planet. Pictured are pale humans with facial hair, orange flowers with green leaves growing right out of dirt under an open sky, and small, colorful metal boxes used for locomotion across vast distances.

Innocent youngers rock back and forth, not caring how they look, in time with the drums. The Zaquens, the ancient eldest six, sit comfortably in simple garb and comfortable chairs, honored with permission to skip the pageantry and just be present.

Our rarest foods and drinks are brought

forward and served, enough only for the Zaquens to taste—a morsel of chocolate, a tiny sip of wine, dried real fruits preserved in stasis. The rest of the adults sip from titanium flagons of fresh spirits and await the cue—the eldest of the elders, with the slightest gesture, silencing all and beckoning us with a single spoken word of invitation:

"Listen."

And we do.

But—I have a confession. I understand that Remembrance brings joy to the Zaquens. And I love seeing the gliders up there, tasked with the job of showing our hearts how to soar. And yet, I admit it... my mind drifts. These old stories, the reverence elders have for cars and oceans and 'open air agriculture...' I know that I am meant to feel a yearning deep in my soul. I was born marked by destiny to take on these beloved memories as if they were my own and carry them safely forward to next year.

But my heart? It is tethered right here. This planet, Tranquility, is just fine by me. Terra, with all her trappings, is meant to be a fairytale world, but to me, it looks like a dusty old textbook ready for recycling. Perhaps this is because I am the oldest of the New Children and, at 15, not so much a child. All my true memories are the delights of Tranquility.

Or perhaps it is because the Remembrance Days of my youth were such simple affairs: a braided bread, an upraised silver cup, but never an entire day of rest. We didn't have flyers yet; we only walked. The elders told the stories and showed the pictures. I strove to show respect. But my mind drifted back to the joys of the Gan Zome, where my Avmis would work while I played. We end the Remembrance Day recitation the same way now as then:

"One year, back on Terra."

I say it, too, because it is a call-and-response prayer, and this is what we do. But my heart is here. And I have seen the other pictures, all the ones they do not show on Remembrance Day. I know now it was those bright metal boxes, 'cars,' that ate up all the air there so they couldn't have their nice green plants under open skies anymore.

Tranquility would never let that happen!

My mind drifts and slips, I wish to be up there in a Flyer or back in the Gan, but I hang on because it is my role, and I am to be a role model for the other New Children. I arrange my face in a way that I hope looks rapt, and I give thanks that there is one part of the story that I truly love. When they tell about Ari and Estr, my mind alights, and I listen up.

Nobody has pictures of them because they had to live in secret, so in my mind, I can make up the pictures as I like. Ari, hazelnut skin and short, short hair, as strong as they were smart. Estr, short and round, wearing glasses and a lab coat, always making notes. Meeting each other without meeting at first, some silly tech that let them talk but not touch. Ari and Estr, paying attention in a way that people around them weren't. They were the two who knew.

When I was young, I would wander in the Gan and play pretend, imagining I was Ari or Estr, imagining that moment of meeting, finding my bashert. I would know them instantly, they would know me, and together, we would grow up and do something good. I am told I was born destined to carry the stories of the Elders and of the time of Terra. Inside, though, I know otherwise. I was born destined to do something new here, on Tranquility, with a soulmate who shares my calling.

It was Ari, the story goes, who first proposed the vision. And it was Estr who was the planner. The Zaquens all tell the story just a little differently, how two by two, then twenty by twenty, then two thousand, and then more... how Estr and Ari were there to help and keep the plan and keep the peace, but how they never wanted to be called leaders. And how the plan succeeded. This is the part I love most.

Zaquen Mir is the best teller because they make their voice go quiet as they tell of the planning when things are happening in secret, and then they make their voice go louder when it is time for launch. Also, Mir skips over the long and boring part about how many generations lived out their entire uneventful lives on the ship that brought us here, working and eating tasteless paste, surviving without thriving. When this verse comes, Mir says:

"Yada, yada, yada, you all know this part," so we youngers know we are allowed to laugh, and it will not mean disrespect.

Every single time I hear this story, my stomach goes all funny when it gets to the launch. I wonder if there was someone like me on that ship, maybe someone who'd just turned

15 and who loved looking up at that single pale moon of Terra, who had to go and grow up but who didn't want to go. Who had a heart for their home planet? When Mir does the telling, they take a deep breath, close their eyes, and pause to remember Ari and Estr:

Imagine. This is the moment those two had worked for all their lives.

Every year at harvest, we sing a song for Ari and Estr. I do love the stories of the first years of harvest, the years I can't remember because I was too small. Avmi tells it to me as a bedtime story still, using their scientist farmer voice just how I like it:

"After year three, we began to believe our own data, as the crops flourished and the first Tranquillian children were born healthy. The corn was the best: juicy alternating kernels in vivid hues of blue-green-rose. The taste was out of this world. None of us had ever savored such wholesome sweetness. We'd floss the corn silk from between our teeth while watching dual moons set in a still-unfamiliar sky, hearts and bellies full."

And then another Avmi will chime in, telling more of the story:

"That first harvest was a hymn we all sang together without knowing the tune. The crops succeeded, even the new hybrid fruits. Once we filled our bellies with corn and beans and squash and quill fruit and built zome homes that kept us sheltered from the arid winds, we began to believe we could do this, that we could write a new verse to the story of the people."

Now, these are the stories I want to carry forward, the stories of Tranquility, of home. I know I will sleep well when Avmi ends the one about the first harvest, almost singing it:

"That first corn, ripe and nourishing, that was the taste of hope."

On Remembrance Day, the other New Children squirm, trying to get closer to the Zaquens. They want to see more pictures of Terra, calling out:

"Again, again!"

The New Children always favor the picture of the long metal locomotion machine that Zaquen Jess calls a "train." Jess has a whistle for this part of the story, and they take it out to make a sound they say sounds just like the train:

"Ch-oooo-ooooooooooooooo."

"Ch-oooo-ooooooooooooooo."

"Ch-oooo-oooooooooooooooooo."

It would be rude to put my hands over my ears, but the sound is loud. Everyone else loves it, though; they clap for more.

Another favored picture is the one of primates sitting in hot water. They have even more hair than the humans in the pictures; hair all over their bodies. The creatures frighten me. All of us here are tall and strong from work, and our brown skin never grows hair anywhere. I'm glad because when I see the pictures of the Terran people and primates, I think of how dirty that hair would have been all the time.

I know they washed with water. The Zaquens tell us Terra was a planet of water and that once upon a time; the water was clean. Here on Tranquility, water is the scarcest thing in the world. Looking at those primates, red faces and blue eyelids, sitting with their whole bodies immersed in water, gives me chills I can't explain.

Mir closes their eyes, a signal for quiet. My signal to return to the here and now.

And then came the Termination Times. The trains had no more fuel and stopped running, left to rust in place on useless tracks. All living beings suffered, primates and plants, birds and bacteria, and the people who lived had to live far away from each other in pods or underground. Most of them despaired, and many chose not to go on. They hungered and thirsted, and they knew they had brought these Times upon themselves, so they mourned.

We all respond:
One year, back on Terra.
After five more of those refrains, they begin the verse I think of as mine. I make sure not to move my lips while silently reciting my verse along with Mir. I know every word verbatim, but pride is not a virtue, so I don't let it show.

A beacon of light appeared in the Nets like a new star. At first, Ari was alone. They told stories of a promised land, a New Eden where humans could begin again. More and more listeners tuned in, and night after night Ari's voice brought solace to survivors. The hearers thought it was a fantasy, a few brief moments of forgetting, a momentary escape from the inevitable impending end.

Ari told a story of an Ark. They called it

Shemok and told tales of brave travelers, volunteers who made their way to one place on Terra where, dauntlessly, they gathered to build the Ark. These travelers were called to a place called Kourou, to leave behind their past and everyone they knew and come with every last tool of knowledge their minds could carry.

We all respond:

One year, back on Terra.

And then a second light flared to life on the Nets, and it was good. This was Estr, the harmony to Ari's melody. When Ari called a story, Estr had the response. For every 'what if' and 'perhaps' from Ari, Estr drummed 'we shall' and 'when.'

Ari was the Talmid Chacham, wisdom folded in their shawl, unfurling for all to share, and Estr was the shofar, calling for believers to come. And come they did, all the ages from all the corners of Terra, with nothing left to lose. Why should they not heed a new star, a last gleam of hope?

Ari and Estr remained in their places, hiding, perhaps, moving, perhaps, but weaving the songs and the stories that carried the Builders and the Departers onward. And when Shemok was built, they sang a new story, one that told of seeds and stasis, of stars and the patience of generations with nothing behind them and darkness far ahead.

We all respond:

One year, back on Terra.

Those are the words I know. After that comes the empty times, and all I can do is be glad I am here and that I was not there, then. I have asked Zaquen Mir. I have asked the Avmis. This question burns inside me still. Ari and Ester, left behind to wait for Termination… what became of them? Once they knew Shemok was gone, that their songs had spun my ancestors out into the spiral of whatever fate would bring, what then? The Avmis can't say because they don't know.

Surely, I plead, they traveled to find one another. It must be so, must it not? Was theirs not the greatest act of generosity, the greatest Tikkun Olam in all the worlds, to see a world beyond repair but repair the world by finding a new one and sending the seed-carriers on their way? And would there not be some small terrestrial thanks, at least a chance to face the end but not alone?

I know, I truly know, that this is not the moral of the story. I am to give thanks, to honor and remember those who came before and who voyaged through the vacuum and the endless night so that we can be here today with our corn. But when I can slip away from the zomes and the work and the play, quiet and alone, I sit shiva for Ari and Estr. It cannot be my destiny only to remember. I feel it in my bones: I will look to the future. And when the call comes this time:

One year, back on Terra.

I move my mouth but remain silent.

The Three of Names

A. S. Klatt Diego

Once there was an ineffective blacksmith named Pete who had a pyromaniac daughter called Delilah. Pete always rushed through his jobs repairing stagecoaches and covered wagons so he could read dime novels, which left young Delilah free to experiment in his shop.

"That braid doesn't suit you," Delilah said to her doll, lighting its hair on fire. One by one, she would burn her toys inside the forge. As she grew older, she entertained herself by making explosives and sold household items so she could buy supplies. Her father never bothered her, so long as she didn't destroy anything important.

Eventually, Pete had no customers, and Delilah had run out of things to sell... or eat. She marched onto the front porch, where her father sat in a rocking chair with a tumbler of whiskey and a book. She tore the novel from his hands and ran into the shop, throwing the book into their small safe.

Pete stomped after her. "Give that back!"

Delilah closed the safe and spun the dial. "I changed the combination. You can find out how your book ends when you bring home a paycheck."

"You sound like your mother did before she left." He rounded on her, cheeks flushed and nostrils flaring. "And how come you haven't left yet? You're old enough to work or find yourself a husband."

Delilah had no interest in husbands, so she agreed to look for a job too. Soon after, Pete put on a faded suit and Delilah donned a floral print dress.

As they stepped onto their front porch, Pete turned to her. "You know what? It's our last day of freedom." He pulled out a few bills from his wallet and counted his money. "Let's go out to eat. We can look for work tomorrow."

Delilah's stomach rumbled. "Sounds good to me and my tummy."

Suddenly, they heard horses trotting around the corner. A carriage pulled up in front of their small brick cottage. When the dust cleared, a uniformed driver dismounted and opened the passenger door. A bearded man in a dark suit stepped out from the velvet interior.

It was Randall King, the richest man in town—and their landlord. Pete adjusted his tie. "Good morning, Mr. King. How can I help you?"

Mr. King glowered and marched up the front

steps. "You can help me by paying your rent on time."

Delilah's eyebrows rose, and her father grimaced. "We're hoping to find work tomorrow, sir."

Mr. King towered over them. "My associate offered to buy this property outright." He pulled an envelope from his jacket pocket. "Here's your eviction notice. Effective immediately."

Pete's hands shook as he unfolded the paper. As Mr. King walked down the steps, Delilah realized she had to act fast. "Wait, Mr. King!"

"I don't have time for begging, girl." Mr. King climbed into the carriage. "Take me to the bank," he told the driver.

Delilah stepped in front of the carriage door before the driver could close it. "Did you know I can turn metal into gold?" she asked.

Mr. King's head snapped towards her. "If that were true, you wouldn't look so pitiful."

Delilah crossed her arms. "Not everyone needs to show off."

Delilah heard her father's footsteps behind her. "What are you doing?" he hissed. She elbowed him to stay quiet.

Mr. King glared at her, but Delilah didn't flinch. "Very well. I'll bring a wagon full of iron tomorrow. If you can turn that into gold, I'll forgive your father's debt and let you keep renting this house."

Delilah stammered, "I wish it were that easy. But I need to be close to where the metal comes from. And I need my supplies."

"That won't be a problem. I own a mine. I'll bring my carriage to collect you and your materials. Be ready at sunrise tomorrow." Mr. King nodded to his driver, who pushed Delilah and Pete aside to shut the carriage door.

"What was that about?" Pete demanded after Mr. King's carriage turned the corner.

"I was improvising. I didn't hear you come up with any ideas."

"I'll talk with him tomorrow and make him see reason. Stay out of sight until we sort this out. Now, if you'll excuse me, I need to work so we can pay our rent." Pete sighed and trudged off into town.

The carriage arrived the next day. Mr. King emerged from it, followed by a uniformed guard.

Pete stood on the porch while Delilah

watched from the living room window. Her father's body tensed when Mr. King and the guard approached.

"You didn't really believe what my daughter said yesterday, right?" Pete asked with a tight smile.

"Are you saying she lied? I don't take kindly to liars," Mr. King growled.

"No! She didn't lie. Not exactly," Pete cleared his throat. "Look, I can't let you take my daughter unchaperoned. It's not proper."

"And how do you propose to stop me?" Mr. King asked.

He waved his hand at the guard, who withdrew a pistol from his holster and pointed it at Pete. Delilah raced out the front door.

"It's okay, Dad." Delilah turned to Mr. King. "I just need a minute to pack." Before either man could reply, she ran back into the house. She packed a bag with a pair of dynamite sticks—her two most prized possessions—a hammer, tongs, and bellows. When she stepped out onto the porch, she paused in front of her father, noting his clenched jaw.

Pete embraced Delilah, who rested her head on his warm flannel shirt and breathed in the scent of tobacco. "You're a clever girl. Promise you'll be careful."

"Stop dawdling," Mr. King said.

The driver held the carriage door open while Delilah stepped inside and sat on a bench opposite Mr. King and the guard. Mr. King nodded at her and checked his silver pocket watch. The driver clicked his tongue at the horses. Their hooves clomped against the dirt road, and the carriage lurched forward.

Mr. King opened his leather briefcase and Delilah glanced at a newspaper inside. The headline read "MINERS' STRIKE ENDS!"

"Lazy ingrates." Mr. King huffed. "I won't need them anymore, now that I have you."

Delilah sympathized with the miners, but she stayed quiet. She peered out the window as they traveled into the barren foothills below the mountains. Water cannons sprayed the rock face, washing gravel down into a murky river. She wished alchemy were real. Then greedy people could make as much gold as they wanted without ruining the world for everyone else.

When the carriage finally came to a stop, the driver opened the door for them. Mr. King offered Delilah a hand, which she refused.

Instead, she hoisted her bag on her shoulder and gripped the carriage door for balance as she stepped down. A strong breeze whipped her face and blew pine needles against her hair and dress.

Mr. King led them to the mine's entrance. The pair of guards at the entrance adjusted their shotguns and saluted Mr. King, who nodded as he passed. Then he climbed into a mining cart and sat on its small wooden bench. Delilah clambered in beside him.

Mr. King called out to a couple of miners working nearby. "Hey, you over there! Make yourselves useful!"

The two men dropped their pickaxes on the ground, ran to the cart, and pushed Delilah and Mr. King's cart into the mineshaft. They were silent until one man began coughing. The younger miner stopped and held the cart steady, while the older man hacked into a handkerchief.

"Is he all right?" Delilah asked.

"The air's bad in here," the young man explained as his colleague straightened.

Mr. King snorted. "If you think any other mine is better, go work there."

"I'm fine," the older man answered with a shaky breath.

"Then what are you waiting for?" Mr. King waved his hand at the miners. They bent over to push the cart again.

The light from outside grew dimmer, and soon they could only see by the oil-wick lamps hung on the damp walls. Delilah shivered in the chilly air. Eventually, the minecart stopped outside a thick wooden door. Mr. King strode out and unlocked the door, which swung open on creaky hinges. The miners held up their lamps to illuminate a small storage room filled with wrought iron bars.

Mr. King pointed at a workbench, vise, and anvil in the far corner of the room, where a forge glowed hot and bright.

"If you don't turn the iron into gold by sunrise, you will die," he said.

"You never said you'd kill me!"

"That's a small price for wasting my time." Mr. King gestured at the men. They grabbed Delilah's arms and shoved her inside the room. "I'll be back at six a.m." He tossed his pocket watch toward her and walked away with the miners, swinging the door shut.

Delilah heard the lock click into place. She sat alone for hours, thinking of ways to escape. But every idea was sure to kill her. She could blast open the door with dynamite, but then the roof would collapse. She could attack the guards with a hammer, but they would shoot her. As the time passed, her frustration, fear, and anger grew until she let out a piercing scream. Suddenly, the door sprang open. A small, pear-shaped woman appeared, dressed in a tunic of moss.

"Why have you disturbed my sleep?" the stranger asked in a high-pitched voice.

Delilah squinted and took in the woman's ethereal features. She realized she was gawking and composed herself. "Who are you? How did you get here?"

"I am a mountain sprite, and you're in my home!" The short woman stamped her bare foot. "It's bad enough those miners pound away with their pickaxes all day. Now I've got to hear your wailing at night!"

"Well, I'm sorry to bother you, but the mine owner threatened to kill me unless I turn this iron into gold. As if such a thing were possible."

"I can turn anything into gold," the sprite

bragged. "But why should I help you?"

Hope surged inside Delilah's chest. "I'll give you my necklace."

The sprite eyed the simple chain around Delilah's neck. "That's not my style."

Delilah took inventory of her possessions. She hesitated. Sighing, she reached for her handbag and took out one stick of dynamite and offered it to the mountain sprite.

"I'm sure you've seen the miners use this to clear out rocks," she said. The sprite grabbed it and tossed it from hand to hand with glee. "Be careful not to drop it! And keep it away from heat until you're ready to use it."

The petite woman placed the stick of dynamite in a corner away from the forge, then walked over to the iron bars and tools. She grabbed the tongs, placed a few bars of iron inside the glowing forge, and waited until they shone bright orange. Then she grabbed an iron bar with the tongs and brought it over to the anvil.

She took a deep breath and chanted, "For a bargain, truth be told, I'll turn this iron into gold!" Then she hammered the iron bar. Sparks leaped around her and fizzled on the damp floor. After the third strike, she stepped back to reveal a small golden sculpture of a fox.

Delilah gasped. "How did you do that?"

"Magic."

Delilah crossed her arms. "That's an incredibly vague answer."

The sprite rolled her eyes. "Sometimes I change how people see things by calling them what they aren't." She gestured to the stack of iron bars. "And sometimes I change how things look by calling them what they are."

Delilah considered this. Before she could respond, the little woman took the tongs and grabbed another hot iron bar from the forge. She laid it on the anvil and raised the hammer. Pound, pound, pound, and that iron bar became a golden goose. And so, the sprite continued until she had turned all the iron bars into gold sculptures.

Mr. King appeared at dawn. When he spotted the sculptures, his eyes widened and he gasped.

Delilah smiled. "I did what you asked. Now, will you let me and my dad stay in our home?"

Mr. King scoffed. "Why should I do that when I could have so much more gold?" He and two guards led Delilah into a larger mineshaft that held a bigger room filled with even more bars of iron.

"Sculpt the iron into gold before sunrise if you want to live," he said, before he slammed the door shut behind him.

Trapped alone inside a room again, Delilah cursed. Again, the sprite unlocked the door and stepped inside. "What'll you give me if I turn this into gold for you?" she asked.

"Another stick of dynamite," Delilah answered. She pulled the second explosive out of her handbag and passed it to the sprite, who giggled with delight.

The sprite placed the iron bars inside the forge and repeated her chant. She worked throughout the night until she had made a gleaming gold menagerie.

At daybreak, Mr. King came back. Golden statues of deer, bears, and mountain lions glowed in the lamplight. Mr. King clapped at the sight.

"Will you let me go now?" Delilah asked.

In response, he brought her to an even larger room with iron bars piled high above her head. "Transform this metal tonight," ordered Mr. King. "If you can do that, I'll marry you and become the richest man in the world!"

When Mr. King left, Delilah finally allowed herself to cry.

The sprite appeared once more. "What will you give me if I shape this metal for the third time?"

"I could give you the pocket watch on the bench." The sprite scowled, so Delilah continued. "Or these tools." She opened her bag and dug around, spotting a small bottle. "And this flask of whiskey."

The sprite inspected the rusted equipment and cheap liquor. "No, those don't interest me."

"I don't have anything else."

"Then promise when you marry Mr. King, you'll give me your first child."

Delilah paled at the idea of having children with Mr. King. She didn't want to marry that greedy bastard! He'd never stop wanting gold from her.

"Why would you bargain for a child?"

The sprite crossed her arms. "Is it strange to want a family?"

Delilah looked closer at the short-haired woman. The sprite straightened her spine and held Delilah's gaze. They were standing so close Delilah could hear the sprite's breath shake as she inhaled. Delilah stepped back. The sprite was cute, but that whole firstborn-child pitch left a sour taste in Delilah's mouth. It reminded her too much of a bedtime story her father had told her.

"You never said your name," Delilah said.

The sprite shrugged. "I don't tell anyone my name."

"Then give me three chances. If I can guess your name, you will do what I say to help me escape from this mountain."

"And what happens if you don't guess my name after three tries?" The sprite raised her eyebrows.

"Then you can have my first kid." Delilah cringed.

"Deal." The two shook hands, and the sprite grinned as if she had already won.

"Are you Lucifer?" Delilah asked.

The sprite looked aghast. "How could you say that, after everything I've done for you?"

"So that's a no."

"Second guess?" The sprite looked smug.

"Is your name Dame Gothel... like the one

who trapped Rapunzel?"

"Nope!" The sprite bounced on her bare feet.

Delilah racked her brain for a name. After several minutes, she asked, "Then is your name... Rumpelstiltskin?"

The sprite's face contorted in rage. "Who told you that?"

Delilah smirked. "Let's just say you have a reputation."

In a fury, Rumpelstiltskin kicked the wall and fell to the ground, screaming in pain. The big toe on her right foot bent at an unnatural angle. Delilah figured the bone was broken. She offered Rumpelstiltskin the flask of whiskey, and the sprite drank half the bottle in one gulp. When Rumpelstiltskin had calmed, Delilah went to the forge. She melted several bars of iron and used her hammer to fashion the metal into rough crutches.

Rumpelstiltskin practiced walking with her new crutches. Meanwhile, Delilah gathered handfuls of dust from the floor and shook it into her purse. She glanced at the pocket watch on the workbench.

"We only have a few hours before sunrise," she said. "You promised you'd follow my plan to escape."

Rumpelstiltskin frowned. "Fine. What do I have to do?"

"First, unlock this door. I know you can do it."

Rumpelstiltskin grumbled, but she balanced on her crutches and picked the lock. Delilah grabbed her bag and a lamp. She opened the door and looked around. They were alone in the mineshaft. The sprite tucked the two sticks of dynamite into her tunic and hobbled after Delilah. They followed the tracks until they saw the faint blue light of pre-dawn from the mine's entrance.

"We don't have long," Delilah said. She gestured for the sprite to follow her. They crept along the cold tunnel wall until they heard the voices of two guards and felt a breeze blowing in the outside air. They moved close to the guards.

"When I throw this dust into the air, I need you to turn it into gold, and I'll blow it past the guards," Delilah whispered. She tossed a handful of dust toward their heads. Rumpelstiltskin murmured something as the wind whipped the dust around, and the dust became gold flecks shimmering in the air.

Delilah pulled the bellows from her bag and squeezed the handles to puff air at the dust.

"What the hell is that?" the nearest guard asked.

"It shines like gold!" the other guard answered. Delilah pumped the bellows harder and blew the glittering flakes of gold down the hill.

The guards deserted their posts to reach for the gold specks. When they were far enough away, Delilah and Rumpelstiltskin fled the mine. They scrambled behind a nearby boulder.

"Your plan actually worked," the sprite said, gazing at Delilah with respect.

"We're not done yet. Mr. King needs to think I'm dead. Otherwise, he'll look for me." Delilah held out her lamp, removed the top, and adjusted the fuel until the flame leaped up above the glass. Luckily, it was too early for the miners to be at work yet. "I need you to light the sticks of dynamite and toss them into the mine."

"But that dynamite is mine!"

"You promised to do what I said."

"I can't throw well. I'm injured."

"Then give me the dynamite." Delilah held

out her hand.

The sprite pouted but gave her the first stick of dynamite. Delilah lit it and tossed it into the gaping hole at the front of the mine. A moment later, she lit the second stick of dynamite and threw it even further.

The young woman and the sprite crouched behind the boulder. An earth-shaking boom echoed in their ears. The air filled with smoke and a moment later, the mineshaft collapsed. Rocks crumbled, piling on top of one another until they spilled out of the tunnel.

"Let's go!" Delilah yelled, ears ringing. She wrapped Rumpelstiltskin's arm over her shoulder. The sprite leaned against her while they climbed up the rocky hillside.

"What are you going to do next?" Delilah asked.

Rumpelstiltskin gazed up at the mountain's peak. "Since you blew up my old home, I need to find a new place to live."

Delilah's cheeks turned pink. She cleared her throat. "I could make dynamite to keep the miners away from your new home."

The sprite's mouth quirked up. "Alright. As long as you finally let me sleep."

Queen of Void

Kayla Al-Shamma-Jones

"Over time, Laura will fade."

That's what Mike—excuse me, Dr. Edmonds—would like me to write in this notebook, over and over again, until I can get the message through my thick skull: *over time, Laura will fade.*

Mike adjusted his starched collar and steepled his fingers under his chin. He thought I hadn't noticed the graduation photo on his desk, with just Laura and him. "Start with fifty times. Most patients write their mantras a hundred, two hundred times during their cognitive restructuring exercises, but I like to start small."

Cognitive restructuring exercises. I fingered the pen I'd stolen from his desk. What a stupid term to describe writing crap down in a one-credit notebook. Leave it to the geeks and gobs of the world to complicate a man's misery.

"I recommend engaging in these cognitive restructuring exercises twice daily," he said. "Once in the morning, once before bed, and... anytime the persistent ideation regarding Laura occurs."

The pen creaked beneath my grip. I felt hot, like all the air had turned to fire. I thought of Laura, spaghettified, stretched into infinite nothingness. But that can't be right. Laura was meticulous, perfect; she color-coded her goddamn diary entries. Blue was for sad days, yellow was for happy, green was for good relationship days, and red was for days when we had a fight. She would never let herself get too close to the event horizon. She was alive. She had to be.

"Laura is not a persistent ideation," I said.

My voice sounded like a low growl, feral and strange in my ears, and then I heard Mrs. Traynor from third grade saying, "this is no way to talk to a friend."

Mike leaned back and cleared his throat. His eyes darted to the right—just a flash, but unmistakable. I'd made him uncomfortable, maybe even scared. I grinned. Fucker deserved to feel awful for giving up on Laura.

Then, Mike leaned forward, pushed his dumb round glasses up his nose, and said: "You do know that she's gone, right?"

I bowed my head and looked down at my fingers. I did not want to be there. I did not want to be anywhere except with Laura.

"Like, *gone* gone. What you see out there is just the light that escaped before she slipped over the event horizon. It's not her."

The contents of my stomach (microalgae soup, a melon-flavored energy drink) tumbled and lurched. I reached out a hand to steady myself on the corner of Mike's pebbly plastic desk. He wants me to admit that Laura has

(don't say it don't think it, don't even)

died

The word felt concrete in my gut. I wanted to think of something else—happier times when Laura was here, and we were in love. . .

"Remember when Laura dragged us both to that zero-g concert?" I asked.

Mike grinned. "God, how could I forget? Those Martians *killed* Bach."

"Remember that stupid foam finger she bought and how she threw it up in the air during the crescendo . . .?"

Mike laughed. "Jesus, I'd forgotten! That damn thing nearly took out half the audience." I chuckled. "She tended to forget about pesky things like gravity and money and, you know, us."

"Yeah." Mike shook his head and smiled. "Good thing it was made of foam."

I liked to imagine that, for a moment, we were both remembering Laura's laughter echoing in the spherical concert hall, the strange, warped notes of gravity-free music surrounding us, the three of us tumbling in slow motion as we tried to catch her runaway souvenir.

"She always did love those damned concerts, though," I said.

Mike's smile faded. He turned to his monitor and began to type.

"I'm going to up your prescription. One hundred milligrams of sertraline and ten milligrams of zalepon at night to help you sleep. Plus another two weeks' bereavement.

I caught the flash of something—longing? regret?—in Mike's eyes, but only for a moment.

I was just a lowly security officer, badge number 4172, clearance level Gamma. I checked IDs at airlocks and patrolled empty corridors at 0300 hours. I wasn't the sorta guy who got to make decisions or petition for resources. But Mike? He was Dr. Edmonds now, with his starched collar and his fancy title. He could walk into Captain Allen's office, pull some strings, and get us the Nebula for a rescue mission if he wanted to. If he cared enough.

The thought burned in my chest, bitter as battery acid. I stood and paced in tight circles before slamming my fists back on Mike's desk.

"How long are we gonna fucking do this, Mike?"

Mike's fingers stopped typing. He froze.

"She's out there," I said. "I can see her ship from the window above my fucking bed."

Mike rubbed his eyes. "John, please. This is hard for both of us."

I crossed my arms over my chest. "Then why am I the only one petitioning for the Nebula?"

"We've been over this, John."

"We could rescue her if we had the Nebula."

Mike sighed. "Captain won't authorize."

"Well," I said. "Well, Captain is a dick."

Mike made a fist and tapped his desk. Once, twice, three times. He pressed his lips together and exhaled.

"It's pointless," Mike said. "She went past the event horizon. Even if Captain authorized it, all we'd find is nothing because she's gone." He leaned forward in his chair, his face flushed, raw. A single jagged vein on his forehead pulsed.

When he spoke again, his voice came in fits and gasps.

"You fucking know as well as I do what happens when someone goes past the event horizon. It grabbed her, and it spaghettified her or ripped her to bits or... God!"

His voice cut out. I felt my own throat constrict.

"Mike..."

"I'm sorry. That was unprofessional of me. I'll see you next week?"

Bringing someone back from a black hole is impossible. True. But I also knew this: I could achieve the impossible, with or without Mike.

One Year, Two Months Before

Mike tells me it might help to write about things I remember, too. Things Laura and I shared. There's one memory that won't leave me alone.

One night, during our honeymoon on a beach resort on the purple sands of Proxima 8, Laura attempted to explain her work aboard *The Gatticus* to me in the simplest possible terms.

"Imagine," she'd said, "two tardigrades."

I felt my entire body droop when she said this. Proxima 8 was a remote planet in a distant arm of the Canis Major Dwarf Galaxy. It was cheap and out of the way, which is why I was able to reserve the whole planet for us—and only us. I sighed, letting my head fall back onto the towel. So much for a romantic evening

"Sure," I said.

"You know what tardigrades are?"

I groaned. "Of course. Water bears, right? Microscopic little dudes? Kinda ugly?"

"Ugly is in the eye of the beholder, but . . yeah. Tiny, too. So tiny, they operate according to the laws of quantum mechanics rather than Newtonian physics."

"Um," I said.

She hoisted herself up on an elbow and lifted her head. If I didn't know any better, I might think she was talking to one of the moons, not me.

"My goal is to use their quantum properties by pairing them with nanochips for instant interstellar communication."

I blinked. "You lost me."

"Okay, okay. Imagine you've got two teeny-tiny containers."

I nodded.

"And in each container, you place one tardigrade and one nanochip. Plus, the two nanochips are entangled."

"Entangled?"

"You know. Change the state of one, change the state of the other."

I blinked.

She began to speak quickly. "The cool thing about tardigrades is that, because they're so small, they can enter a state of quantum entanglement with each other, even if you destroy the computer chips afterward. Plus, they can survive anything. Even black holes!"

I closed my eyes. At that point, I'd given up on understanding.

"Cool," I said.

"Which means . . one day, we could see what's on the other side of the event horizon."

She paused there.

"John?"

I squinted up at her. She leaned over me, her lavender hair cascading in my face.

"Hmm?" I said.

She smiled down at me. "Were you listening?"

***

Dammit.

If I had listened, I might have known how to save her. Maybe I could have rescued her before she became whatever she is now.

Laura. I'm so, so sorry.

Three Weeks, One Day After

After my session with Mike, I wandered through the dim corridors. Most everyone else was asleep. I should have been, too. But I wasn't. I rarely slept in those days. I rarely ate, too. With Laura gone, I had become a walking corpse drifting through the world of the living. My days always, always ended at 0200 hours with me standing in front of Laura's lab.

I fished her keycard out of my pocket, then looked both ways. There was nobody. I scanned the card. The door hissed open, releasing a rush of familiar scents—sterile chemicals and a lingering whisper of sandalwood. I inhaled deeply, desperately, as if I could capture her essence in my lungs. One breath, two, three ... My chest burned, but I held on, afraid to let even this tiny piece of her escape.

Finally, my lungs rebelled, forcing out the air in a rush. As the scent faded, reality crashed back in. I was here for a reason. I approached the neat rows of specimens Laura had left behind. Each vial was meticulously labeled and color-coded, paired off like Noah's ark in miniature. One to keep, one to send through the void. She had taken a few with her on that fateful mission. My eyes scanned the labels. There had to be something here, some clue in her notes or meticulous organization, that could lead me to her.

I found a lone specimen, partnerless. I'd never messed with her things before. It felt like sacrilege. But I wanted her back. Needed her. And if Mike wouldn't help me... Well, I had no choice, did I?

I grabbed the sample and slid it under the glass lens of Laura's nanoscope. The nanoscope's controls were a confusing mix of sleek, modern design and archaic levers. I twisted and turned the knobs, feeling like a caveman trying to operate a spaceship. I fumbled with them anyways, twisting and turning the knobs and levers until, finally, an image swam into focus on one of her many monitors. The specimen had a translucent, segmented body with eight stubby legs ending in minute curled claws. Its rounded mouth area was shrunken and lifeless. It was, I knew, in suspended animation. Not dead, but waiting. Just like Laura. All it needed to awaken was a single drop of water.

I searched her lab for a sink, found one, and filled a paper cup with water. This was probably all wrong—Laura would have had some precise instrument for rehydration, but I didn't have time to figure it out. Every second counted. What if her ship was running low on fuel? Oxygen?

I dipped the slide into the beaker with clumsy fingers and carefully placed it back under the nanoscope. My breath caught as I leaned in.

At first, nothing. Then, like a time-lapse of a blooming flower, the tardigrade began to swell. Its shriveled body absorbed the water, expanding and unfurling. I watched, transfixed, as tiny legs twitched and uncurled—life— awakening from suspended animation.

I stood and began to pace. If Laura's theories were right, the tardigrade's quantum-entangled partner on her ship would be stirring, too. A connection across impossible distances. A lifeline.

Minutes crawled by. The tardigrade wiggled on the screen. I paced some more and drummed my fingers on the desk. What now? I'd woken the damn thing, but Laura was still—

If only Laura were here.

My throat tightened. Hot tears burned against my cheeks. God. If only she were here.

"Laura?" I said. "Are you out there? Laura, I miss you."

The tardigrade writhed. The lab felt quiet and infuriating and awful. Then—

A soft whir. The computer had turned on. One of Laura's many monitors clicked on, and a program—a simple word processor, it seemed—opened and maximized itself.

"Holy shit," I whispered.

I leaned closer as a stream of data appeared in the text box. At first, I thought it was noise or else a glitch of some sort. But there was a pattern to it that repeated over and over again: 01001100 01000001 01010101 01010010 01000001

Zeros and ones. I frowned. Even a Security

guy like me knew binary. Binary could be used for all sorts of things. Bits and bytes, but also words.

With trembling fingers, I began to decode.

01001100 = L
01000001 = A
01010101 = U
01010010 = R
01000001 = A

I stared at the letters, scarcely breathing.

A cursor blinked at the end. My fingers hovered over the keyboard, shaking.

I typed: IT'S JOHN. ARE YOU OKAY?

The computer hummed again, then:

01001001 = I

The cursor blinked. I breathed. I. And? There had to be more.

I typed: ARE YOU THERE?

A few seconds passed, then:

01001100 = L
01001001 = I
01010110 = V
01000101 = E

The screen blinked off, plunging the lab into darkness. For a moment, I stood frozen, wondering if I'd imagined it all. Then, a soft whir broke the silence. The printer in the corner sprang to life, spitting out a single sheet of paper.

I lunged for it, my hands shaking so badly I nearly tore the page. There it was, in stark black and white: our conversation. Proof. I ran my fingers over the letters, half-expecting them to vanish at my touch.

How was this possible? Why would Laura communicate in binary? Questions swirled in my mind, but one certainty cut through the chaos: Laura was alive. Somehow, someway, she was out there. And I would move heaven and earth, cross the very fabric of space-time if I had to, to bring her home.

Three Weeks, Four Days After

I've tried to reproduce my results—yesterday, the day before that, maybe even the day before that. I can't tell; time has mushed together into a strange blobby thing. I didn't want help, but fruitless days and nights pushed me towards the inevitable. It was time to call the only Science Officer I knew: Dr. Mike Edmonds.

I messaged him at 1145 this morning (or was

it yesterday morning?), but he didn't respond. And, for a long while, he didn't show, either. I thought that he'd decide that engaging in my delusions was harmful to the processing of my grief or some shrink-y bullshit like that. But at precisely 0200, he arrived.

Mike stumbled in, hair mussed and eyes heavy with sleep. His blue bathrobe—the same ratty thing he'd had at the Institute—gaped open, revealing boxer briefs with a frayed waistband.

"John?" he said.

I thrust the printout at him and watched as his bloodshot eyes scanned the page.

"What is this?" he asked.

"A message, I think."

"From who?"

I scratched my head. Saying it out loud made me feel crazy. I wondered if he'd put me in a straightjacket if I told him what I thought had happened. But I'd called him in to help, hadn't I? How could he help without the truth?

"Who do you think it's from?" I said.

He reread the transcript and said, "Your message said this happened when you rehydrated the tardigrade."

"Yep."

"And that's the specimen there?"

Mike pointed to the tardigrade. It wiggled its legs at us.

"Yep," I said.

"But you haven't been able to replicate it."

"No."

Mike rubbed his chin. "What did you do right before it happened the first time?"

"I sat down in this chair. I rehydrated the specimen. And then I . . .I asked Laura where she was and told her I missed her."

Mike set the transcript down, smoothing it with trembling hands. "I see."

"It's her. It's gotta be," I said.

Mike was silent for a long moment, his eyes flicking between the transcript and the wiggling tardigrade.

"John," he said after a long while. "I . . .I don't know what this is. But it's certainly not nothing."

I stepped toward him. "You believe me?"

Mike thought for a moment. "I believe you experienced... something. I want to help. But we need to approach this systematically. No more late-night secret experiments."

I nodded. All at once, the tension I'd been carrying in my shoulders for weeks seemed to melt away, leaving me light-headed. I steadied myself against the lab bench and took a deep breath.

"Meet me here tomorrow at 2000 hours," Mike said. "I want to conduct a proper experiment. We'll try to replicate your results under controlled conditions."

"Thank you," I said—or did I whisper?

As he turned to leave, Mike paused at the door. "And John? Try to get some sleep. We've got work to do."

Three Weeks, Five Days After

The next day, Mike explained the experiment to me like this:

"Suppose we created a miniature artificial black hole right here, in this lab.

Now, let's also assume that the tardigrade we have here is indeed quantum-entangled with the one on Laura's ship.

The tardigrade on Laura's ship doesn't have its nanochip because it went through the black hole. The tardigrade survived, but the nanochip didn't. But ours does. What would happen if we connected that nanochip to a neural interface?

What if we also connected you, John, to that neural interface?

I think that we could connect the two of you, John. You could see her.

Of course, this would be a very risky experiment. We have some great surgical resources aboard this ship, but I'm not a neurosurgeon. There's a chance I could mess this up.

But if I'm right, you could see her, John. Maybe even talk to her."

"No," he said. "You are her husband. You should be the one to see her."

Four Weeks, Two Days After

We spent the next few nights gathering equipment, running simulations, and arguing over safety protocols. Cups of bitter synthetic coffee replaced sleep.

The familiar space had been transformed into a maze of blinking monitors and humming machines. My heart raced as Mike attached the electrodes to my temples, his fingers cool and steady against my skin.

"Last chance to back out," he said.

I grinned. "Not a chance."

Mike nodded, then flipped the switch.

The air shimmered, and an artificial black hole appeared before us. It was a void so deep it hurt to look at, encircled by a mesmerizing cascade of colors I had no names for. The quantum-entangled tardigrade waved its legs about wildly.

"Initiating neural link," Mike said.

A strange tingling spread through my mind, like pop rocks fizzing behind my eyes. The room began to fade, and reality jolted and then faded.

"You feeling anything?"

Before I could answer, the room faded and was replaced by a floating sensation.

"John?" Mike's voice echoed. "Can you hear me?"

I tried to respond, but my consciousness was already stretching, expanding into the void.

"I'm going in," I thought. Or perhaps I spoke it aloud. I could no longer tell the difference. Actions, thoughts, feelings—all impulses were the same in the unseeing ether of the void.

I pushed forward through layers of light, color, and essence. I could see all of space and time as interconnected threads, glowing with love and light. In that moment, I was everywhere and nowhere, existing in all moments at once. Past, present, and future blurred together in a kaleidoscope of sensation. I saw the birth of stars and their deaths, galaxies colliding in slow-motion ballets. Time ran backward, forwards, and sideways.

***

I'm sorry, notebook.

I know I am supposed to write affirmations in you, to use you as a tool to convince myself that Laura has indeed passed on.

Mike also told me to use you to document what I'm feeling as honestly as possible, so that's what I will do now.

It's hard to explain what happened in the void, but I will do my best.

***

At some point—I'm not sure when—the void

shifted. A form coalesced from the darkness. It was charcoal gray and undulating. It looked like Laura, but not Laura. She had morphed into a bizarre hybrid of woman and tardigrade, familiar yet utterly alien.

"Laura?" My voice echoed strangely in the non-space.

The figure shimmered, transforming from charcoal to liquid silver. "I'm here, John."

"Laura." I felt elated and buoyant; I floated toward her. "I came all this way."

"Stay away."

The oneness shattered. "Why?"

"I've become something else, John. Something more." Her form rippled, eight leg-like appendages rippling.

My body dropped, and my stomach lurched as if I had been pushed.

"I don't understand," I said.

"The black hole didn't destroy me, John. It transformed me. I've merged with it, become one with the fabric of space-time itself."

I felt myself float upwards again.

"I know," I said. "I feel it, too. We can live here together."

"We can't."

"Why not?"

"Live, John." Her form began to fade.

"But I am living! Laura, please—"

She vanished, leaving me alone in the void once more.

"Laura!" I screamed into the emptiness, my voice lost in the infinite expanse of the black hole.

But Laura didn't answer.

The void collapsed around me, reality rushing back into a dizzying flood. I gasped as the harsh fluorescent lights blinded me.

"Thank God," Mike said. "I thought I'd lost you."

Four Weeks, Two Days After

Over time, Laura's memory will fade.
Over time, Laura's memory will fade.
Over time, Laura's memory will fade.
Over time . . .

Sixteen Weeks After

I stood at the viewport, gazing out at the stars. My reflection stared back at me. I had more wrinkles now, especially on my forehead. My hair had turned silver. In my eagerness to see Laura, I'd forgotten that time bends and stretches near a black hole. Five minutes out there, thirty years in there. A thirty-six-year-old man in a sixty-six-year-old body. Another impossible thing to accept.

Laura had been gone for sixteen weeks. Sometimes, I caught myself tilting my head, straining to catch a whisper of her voice. Despite knowing better, I'd turn toward the sound, half-expecting to see her sitting there, smiling, holding a cup of chai with too much creamer (my favorite), inviting me to lay down with her for a while.

My quarter's doorbell interrupted my fantasy. Mike and I had both lost our positions (unauthorized use of lab equipment) and would soon be deposited on the nearest starbase. Until then, Captain allowed him to be both my shrink and my doc.

"Come in," I said.

Mike entered. His shirt was wrinkled, and the top button was undone. His beard had grown wild. His hands, once steady as he took notes during our sessions, now fidgeted with the frayed edge of his sleeve.

"How are you feeling?" Mike said.

"Better," I said. "Clearer, I think. You were right. She's fading for me a little. Or, rather, her human form is."

"Good, I guess." Mike paced and turned in circles. "Maybe. I don't know. I've been thinking about what you saw."

He joined me at the window, and together we stood in silence. I glanced at him, and after a few longing moments, he looked up at me. His eyes were red-rimmed and wet.

"Do you think it was her?" he said.

I gazed out at the stars, my eyes instinctively searching for the patch of space where Laura's ship had vanished. The afterimage that had haunted me for weeks was finally gone, leaving only an unremarkable expanse of darkness. Yet somehow, its absence felt more poignant than its lingering presence ever had.

"I think so," I said.

He nodded, and then neither of us spoke for quite some time.

"I came to say that I'm sorry," Mike said. "For doubting you. For not being the friend you needed."

I smiled, feeling the pull of new wrinkles. "And I'm sorry for pushing you away. For forgetting that you loved her too."

Mike's eyes glistened. "They'll never believe us. About what you saw out there."

"I know."

Mike turned away from me. "Just like I never believed you."

I nudged him lightly with my elbow.

"Don't beat yourself up," I told him. "Over time, the memory of your dickishness will fade."

For the first time in many weeks, Mike laughed.

"I've been trying to follow your advice," I said. "Trying to let go, to move on. It's not easy, but it's helping. Day by day, it's helping." Mike smiled, the corners of his eyes crinkling. "Guess we're both learning."

I returned to the viewport, pressing my palm against the cold glass. The universe sprawled before us, vast and mysterious and filled with possibilities we were only beginning to understand.

"We sure are," I said.

I pulled the notebook from my pocket, the

one Mike had given me weeks ago. I flipped it open to the first page, where I'd scribbled the same phrase over and over.

Mike glanced at it, then back at me. "John..."

I took a deep breath and wrote a single line beneath the others:

"Over time, Laura will fade. But we won't let her be forgotten."

I closed the notebook and tucked it away, my eyes fixed on the stars. Somewhere out there, in the depths of space and time, a part of Laura—my Laura—would never, ever fade.

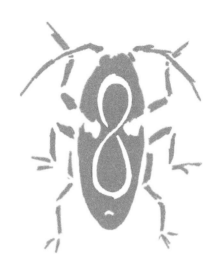

The Metamorphosis of Hans

Laurel Busby

Hans Braun has to go to Terminal 8. Of course, he does. Eight is two little turds joined as one. An infinite loop of turds.

It was on his eighth birthday that his mother died in a car accident while rushing home with the Pokémon cake that he had insisted she buy. His father never forgave him. His eighth-grade year had been a bullying horror show that ended with him repeating the year due to too many absences. On 8-8-2008, the day before he left home for college, his father had screamed at him, "I would shove you in front of a semi if it would bring your mother back to life." Hans should have spent the day under the bed. Too many eights.

Then, eight years ago, his university had allotted him eight years to complete his novel and dissertation. He should have known that he couldn't have done it. Well, he'd done it, but the committee hadn't approved it, which meant the same thing. Eight years of his life spent, and nothing to show for them but failure.

Today would continue the trend. Next to him, in the driver's seat of her Lexus, Rachel frowns as she maneuvers between two haphazardly parked cars at the airport drop-off, then stops beneath a column labeled with a massive 8F.

Eight F. His grade in life.

Hans shoves open the door and steps into the heat. A car horn blares. In front of him, a crud-covered truck belches black exhaust that drifts toward him, then envelops him. He tries to wave it away, but it refuses to dissipate. He flails his arms faster. He can no longer breathe. He can't see. The world has vanished. No, he has vanished. Maybe he should have vanished long ago.

A coughing fit overtakes him, and the exhaust glides away. He gulps fresher air. His trembling hands fall to his side. A TSA agent squints at him and takes a step in his direction. He lumbers to the back of Rachel's car. The latch clicks, and he pops the trunk.

Inside, his belongings ooze ugliness. Two massive beige suitcases passed down through his family for decades, a grimy carry-on he found by the dumpster last week, and a fraying backpack holding three translations of *The Metamorphosis* by Franz Kafka plus his laptop with the drafts of his dissertation and novel. He had pitched everything else he owned in the trash.

He should have rid himself of the dissertation and novel too. According to his committee chair, Professor Augustine Mettles, both belonged with L.A.'s detritus. She urged him to delete the dissertation, "*Metamorphosis*: A Neoclassicist Reduction of Speculative Tropes," from his hard drive and start again—as if he could afford to spend another eight years on such an endeavor. She added that his *Metamorphosis*-inspired novel "lacked the creativity, dark humor, and insight of *Metamorphosis*." She also called it "derivative," "convoluted," and "suffocating." Afterward, standing outside the door, he overheard her dub it the dullest student novel she had ever read.

He glances at Rachel. Wind dances through her hair as she rounds the car to him. She smiles with compassion, and her flecked green eyes meet his with kindness and warmth. He can't have that. Perhaps he should spit on her. That would erase any feelings of tenderness. No, the wind would probably take the spit and throw it back in his face.

Rachel hugs herself, opens her mouth as if to speak, and then closes it. What could she say?

Her novel, which she produced in only four years while simultaneously completing 60 units of Ph.D. coursework, was praised as "transformational" and "wildly inventive" by her committee. It had already caught her an agent and three offers from top publishing houses. She expects to have a deal before his plane lands. She has even been offered an associate professorship in New York City while he has to go to Portland to sponge off a father who still hates him. Tears threaten. He turns a mental blowtorch on them, and they recede.

Rachel holds up a book of matches. "After you fell asleep last night, I found these." She lifts the cover to unveil her scribbled name and phone number—a memento from their chance meeting at the Eight Ball bar four years ago, when he was a grad program veteran and she had just been accepted into the program. On that day, he had completed the last final exam for his Ph.D. coursework, and was about to begin his novel and dissertation, while she had looked forward to her first semester of classes. They talked about *Metamorphosis*, his inspiration, and Rachel expressed admiration for his novel premise and dissertation idea. He hadn't been sure about either, but her enthusiasm convinced him to move forward. This matchbook marks the beginning of their doomed relationship. It also memorializes the moment he swerved from promising student to colossal failure.

He stuffs them into his pocket. "A momentous night," he says.

"It was." A sheen of wetness blooms in her eyes.

He looks away. "I better go."

She leans forward to hug him. He compels his body to reciprocate and forces out some polite words. "Good luck in New York, Rachel … with your book and job."

"Thank you. Good luck too … with your trip."

***

At the end of the gangway, dressed in a flight attendant's uniform, Rachel waves from the airplane door.

Hans jerks to a stop and gapes. Somebody plows into the back of him. He stumbles into his carry-on bag, which teeters and begins to fall. He reaches for the handle, loses his balance, and struggles to right himself. He can't. He falls, lands on all fours, smacking his palms and knees into the metal floor.

"Sorry, sir," a woman with a smoker's voice says from behind him. "I wasn't expecting you to stop."

Rachel's legs hurry toward him. She's wearing stockings and short blue heels. He didn't know that Rachel owned stockings and short blue heels.

"Are you hurt?" she says.

Pain reverberates through his body. His knees bore into the diamond-plate aluminum floor. "Let me help you, sir." Rachel reaches a hand out to him.

He ignores it, sucks in some air, and pushes himself to his haunches. He stares at his toppled carry-on bag. Rachel takes the handle and rights it, then stretches her hand out to him again.

He looks up at her. "What are you doing here?"

"What do you mean?" She takes one step back and drops her hand to her side. She wears mascara and golden eye shadow. Rachel abhors makeup. This woman's neck is long. Too long.

He peeks at her name badge. Rachel.

"What's your last name?" he says.

She doesn't answer and retreats to the plane door.

It must not be his Rachel. That Rachel had driven off in a Lexus. That Rachel wasn't a flight attendant. That Rachel also wasn't his anymore. Sweat pools under his arms, and his feet slide in his sandals. A smell rises from both areas. He gets to his feet, adjusts his backpack, and takes hold of his rolling carry-on.

"Sorry," he says as he passes flight attendant Rachel. "I thought you were someone else."

She nods and says, "No problem," but her eyes don't mean it.

A blush slides up his neck and across his face. He turns and heads down the aisle toward his window seat—27A, but when he reaches it, he finds a tiny kid there, clutching a red crayon and zipping it back and forth across a notebook.

"That's my seat," he tells the kid.

A pony-tailed woman sits in the next seat. She's doing something on her phone and doesn't look up as she says, "Not anymore. They moved you."

"I don't want to move."

"You got an upgrade."

"I don't want an upgrade."

The woman glances at him, then back to her phone. "Tough."

Flight attendant Rachel strides down the aisle, her hair slicing back and forth with each step.

"You're in 8F." She enunciates the number and letter as if speaking to a kindergartner. Her mouth opens wide, and she pronounces it again in loud, slow motion. "8 … F."

"No."

The word lashes out of him, and all chitchat on the plane ceases. Heads crane over seats and into the aisle to peer at him.

"You didn't pay to lock in your seat, so the airline has the right to change it at any time," Rachel says.

The pony-tailed mom aims her phone camera at him and begins to record.

"I won't move," he says.

"Yes, you will. Follow me." Rachel spins around and heads toward the front of the plane.

A muscle flexes in his jaw, and heat suffuses his face. The mom raises an eyebrow. A gleeful smile quirks her lips. He turns around and follows Rachel to 8F.

It's an aisle seat next to an empty window seat. He reaches for the handle of the overhead compartment, but Rachel puts her hand on the door to keep it closed.

"It's full. You'll have to check your bag."

She gives him a tag to claim it later, then wheels it away.

"Hans Braun!" A sturdy, squat woman in a black-and-white-checked blouse strides down the aisle towards him. No. It can't be. A smile blossoms across her features. It hits him like a slap. "Headed to Seattle too?"

He shakes his head, and his stomach clenches. No. Clenches is too tame a word. A vengeful beast has spawned in his gut, and it's ripping him apart. An urge to scream crawls up and through him. No. He must suppress it. He must think. He can't lose control. Besides, this can't be real. This has to be another confusing doppelgänger, but Professor Mettle doesn't transform into anyone else. She soldiers toward him and points at her ticket. 8G.

"Looks like we're seatmates." She squeezes past him and settles in the window seat, then shoves a briefcase under the seat in front of her and pulls down the window shade.

As though obeying an order at gunpoint, Hans slides off his backpack, stows it, and sits beside her. Prof. Mettle twists to face him. "So, what's next for you?"

He can't tell her he's going back to Portland to hide in his childhood bedroom, but there's nothing else to say. He shrugs.

"Perhaps I can help you," she says.

He chokes out a sound halfway between "um" and "ugh.'

"First novels are often trash, Hans." The tips of her fingers alight on his arm, and he forces himself not to fling them away. "Robert Louis Stevenson burned the first version of *Dr. Jekyll and Mr. Hyde* after harsh criticism, you know."

Rachel's voice comes over the loudspeaker. She gives the standard boarding announcement about not smoking, fastening one's seatbelts, and turning off electronic devices. She holds up an oxygen mask, demonstrates how to use it, then says that safety materials are in the back of the in-flight magazine. To block out further conversation with Prof. Mettle, Hans snatches the magazine out of the seat back in front of him. It features a picture of an eight of clubs with a man at its center who oddly resembles Hans himself and is being sucked into the depths of a massive whirlpool. A title underneath reads, *The Metamorphosis of Hans*, by Franz Kafka.

Professor Mettle peers at it. "How curious," she says.

He shifts his back to her and turns the page, expecting an ad or maybe a table of contents, but instead, he sees a story, *The Metamorphosis of Hans*.

I

As Hans Braun awoke one morning from uneasy dreams, he found
himself transformed in his bed into a monstrous vermin.

A trembling takes root in him, so severe that it reminds him of the moment he learned his mother was dead. His mom's friend Lily, an emergency room doctor, had phoned. She was sobbing and asking to talk to his father, but he told her that his father couldn't talk. He was downstairs working at the convenience store. Lily said there had been an accident. Hans asked if his mom was okay, and she whispered that she was gone.

"It was nobody's fault," she said. How could it be nobody's fault? His mom had been driving the car. Someone else had been driving the other car. And it was his 8th birthday that had pushed her out the door. Somebody, many somebodies, were at fault. An earthquake tumbled through his body then, and it reverberated again as he read the sentence, a sentence he knew well, the first sentence of *Metamorphosis*, except that it featured his name instead of the protagonist's.

He glares at his name, trying to shift it to what it should be, Gregor Samsa, but it won't shift. Instead, it pulses at him. Hans. Hans. Hans. Like a malfunctioning neon sign. The rest of the story continues down the page and onto the next and the next and the next, except that every place that should say Gregor, now says Hans. The tale is otherwise unaltered. The main character has awakened as a six-foot cockroach. The other characters wish they could squash him beneath their shoes.

He closes the magazine and glances at Professor Mettle. She raises an eyebrow and smiles. "Anything interesting in there?"

She must think this is a grand joke. She obviously stuffed the magazine in the seat-back pocket when she took her seat. He yearns to tell her what he thinks of her joke, but his throat feels dry and full, like someone crammed gauze down it, so he shifts his back to her with a shake of his head. Maybe he should muster the strength to act like her joke was funny, laugh, and say, "Good one." But the humiliation is too raw, and the magazine cover taunts him. The man swirling into the eddy has the distraught face of someone about to be sucked into a sewer, and Hans feels like he's looking into the mirror. How could Professor Mettle think this was funny? How could she flush his last eight years of labor down the proverbial toilet and then create a magazine to memorialize the event?

Perhaps he should get off the plane. It hasn't taken off. He could have a tantrum, say he was petrified to fly, and be escorted back to the airport. The plane jerks forward, shoving him into his seat, and then careens along the runway. Too late. A thin geyser of bile erupts into the back of his throat. He closes his eyes and grips the spine of the magazine. The bile in his throat rises higher. A bit slides across his tongue. He paws through the seat pouch for the vomit bag, jerks it open, and holds it to his mouth.

"Nervous flyer, eh?" Prof. Mettle says.

He orders himself to think of nothing but the bag and his breath. There is no Prof. Mettle. He didn't lose his girlfriend and fail to achieve his Ph.D. A version of *Metamorphosis* starring himself as a roach had not appeared in his in-flight magazine. After the plane finishes its ascent, a beep sounds. His eyelids flick open. At the front of the aisle, Rachel unbuckles her seatbelt and walks into the galley. He unbuckles himself.

"The seatbelt light is still on," Mettle says.

He stands up anyway. He keeps the bag to his mouth with one hand and clutches the magazine to his chest with the other. He rushes down the aisle, away from Rachel, to the rear restrooms. He yanks the door open and disappears inside.

The pale room with its bright white light is medicinal, antiseptic, like a shrunken hospital bathroom. Hans sits on the toilet and tries to calm himself. Maybe he was just seeing things. He opens the magazine. His name winks at him. He's a cockroach headed for an ignominious death. It's as if one of his nightmares from the past eight years has come true, and he has actually awakened as a giant insect. What if …

His gaze whips to the mirror. He sees his puffy, sleep-deprived face, his lank, unbrushed hair, his pale body with its sprinkling of freckles. He could be a ghost or a zombie, maybe. But he's not a bug. Not yet.

He crushes the magazine closed. A ripping sound startles him. He's gripped the magazine's cover so hard that it's torn, right across his cartoon face. The image no longer looks like him. It could be anybody. It could be Prof. Mettle. A half-smile twitches across his lips.

But his name still adorns the cover. *Hans* in big, bold courier type. He tears off the word, stuffs it in his mouth, and begins to chew. The flavor is corrosive. A sharp, slick paper adorned in inks that could kill someone if consumed in enough quantity. He spreads his legs and spits the wad into the toilet. It hits the bottom with a wet ping and sits in a tiny amount of liquid.

He stands and flushes. A flap snaps down, suction roars, and his masticated name disappears. A smile flits across his face, but then slides away. The rest of the magazine still exists. He sets it on the aluminum counter and tears off the cover, rips it in half, then takes those pieces and rips them in half again. He does this over and over again, eight times, until all that remains are shreds not much bigger than confetti. He drops them in the toilet, then flushes. A vacuum blast takes the offending remnants away, and a little bubble of satisfaction bounces around his heart.

He takes hold of the next page and does the same thing. Then he rips up three pages at once, then three more, then four, and flushes again and again and again.

A knock sounds on the door. "Sir, are you all right in there?"

"Be out soon."

Giddiness spreads through him as he tears and tears and tears and flushes and flushes and flushes until it's gone. Literally down the drain. That magazine won't be bothering him anymore. He floats out of the bathroom, beams at Rachel at the far end of the aisle where she tends her drink cart, and does a little skip on the last step to his seat.

Prof. Mettle flips through the in-flight magazine on top of her tray table. "Look Hans. *The Metamorphosis of Hans.* Did you know I'd be sitting with you? What an odd duck you are."

Her skin has a waxy quality that is not quite human, and her rosy cheeks vibrate. She looks like an ebullient apple. She chortles and taps his knee with the magazine. He takes hold of it and flips through it. It's exactly like his.

A few rows back, a mother ushers two children toward the bathroom. Gripping the magazine, he moves toward their seat row. He pretends to trip, stumbling into their empty seats. As he recovers his feet, he withdraws the three copies of their in-flight magazine. He flips through each one. *The Metamorphosis of Hans. The Metamorphosis of Hans. The Metamorphosis of Hans.*

He counts the seat rows, at least 20 with seven seats per row, plus first-class seats, more than 150 passengers. Could each have this hellish version of *Metamorphosis* as their in-flight magazine? He couldn't flush them all down the toilet. Or could he?

"Hi," he says to a trio of middle-aged travelers watching movies in the next row. "I'm collecting in-flight magazines. These are misprints, and we'll be replacing them with a new magazine."

They hand him their magazines, each one featuring his face in a panicked swirl. As he progresses down the aisle, more and more people give him their magazines. When he's hefting at least 60 of them, he heads to the bathroom. The mother and her two children tumble out of one lavatory, and he goes in. He sets the magazines on the counter and begins tearing the top one up, dropping the pieces into the toilet. He flushes. The toilet roars, and the papers disappear.

He tears up a second magazine and flushes. He demolishes a third and a fourth, and they vanish down the drain. On the eighth magazine, he pulls the handle, but there's no snap and roar. He tries again. Again nothing. Maybe it's jammed. He grabs a paper towel and uses it to pull shreds out of the toilet bowl. He stuffs them in the trash, then flushes again. The flap at the base of the bowl still doesn't release. He pulls out more and more shreds, until only eight tiny pieces float in the small puddle of liquid. He pushes the handle, shakes it, smacks it, but the catch won't release.

He grabs some paper towels, shoves them in the toilet bowl, and pushes at the stuck flap. It doesn't move. He sticks his foot in the toilet, stomps on the flap. Nothing. Stymied, he flops onto the toilet seat.

Perhaps the toilet isn't necessary for the disposal. He peeks into the trash bin. It's mostly empty. He picks up a magazine, rips off the cover and the first few pages, tears them in half, and stuffs them into the bin. He drops the rest of the magazine on top of them. He does this again and again, shoving torn magazine after magazine into the bin. With the final one, the bin is so stuffed that it can barely close.

He exits the bathroom and finds that Rachel and her drink cart have come so far down the aisle that he can no longer get to his seat. The flight attendants in the other aisle complete their refreshment journey and head back to the mid-plane galley. The magazines in their aisle wink at him from their pockets. He switches to that aisle and begins collecting more magazines. When his arms are full, he turns around and heads to the bathrooms.

Rachel spies him. "Sir, what are you doing?"

He keeps walking.

"Excuse me a moment," Rachel says to her fellow flight attendant, and strides down the aisle toward the rear of the plane.

Hans reaches a lavatory, but its red occupied latch has been thrown. Two of the other bathrooms are also occupied. The only one that's left is the one with the trash bin that he's already filled. Rachel storms toward him. He pushes open the door and locks himself inside.

She pounds on the door.

"Sir."

"I feel sick. Diarrhea. Can't talk."

He sits on the toilet with the stack of magazines in his lap. He fakes a loud groan of pain.

"Sir, we'll need those magazines back."

He hugs them closer. He groans again. He mimics the rushing sound of a loud, wet bowel movement, then groans a third time. Maybe she'll leave, then he can dart into a different bathroom and get rid of the magazines.

"Sir, I'm not leaving until you open this door."

Of course not. From his throne, he

investigates the various bathroom cabinets, but none could stow dozens of magazines. An ache in his right butt cheek makes him wriggle to get more comfortable, and he remembers that the pocket isn't empty. He reaches inside it and pulls out Rachel's book of matches. Its silvery blue cover shimmers. He strokes it, an electric shiver slides up his hand to his heart. He opens the matchbook. Inside are 20 unused matches. They gleam.

He sets down the stack of magazines and brings one into his lap. He runs his hand across it and clutches his shiny matchbook in the other. Across from him, above the bathroom door, a smoke detector glistens. He rips the back cover off the magazine and stuffs it into the smoke detector's vent.

He tears off the magazine's front cover, crumples it into a ball, and tosses it into the sink. He does the same with the next page, then drops the magazine to the floor. He picks up another copy and does the same thing. He keeps going until more than half are missing their cover and first page. The sink overflows with balls of paper. He lights a match and places it against a ball of paper. It ignites.

Inky smoke rises in a thin line toward the ceiling. As the paper burns, he rips off more magazine covers and title pages, dropping the balls onto his little bonfire until all the magazines have been relieved of their first pages. A wailing alarm squeals from the smoke detector. Someone bangs on the door.

"Open up!"

The door's latch begins to slide open. Hans shoves it closed and holds it in position. With his other hand, he covers his mouth with his shirt. Dark smoke envelops the room. His eyes burn.

A man outside shouts, "Move away from the door!"

Hans leans into it instead. A body slams the door. The shock shutters through him, but he remains pressed against the door, holding it in place. Another crash. Another shutter. A slam, and the door craters inward. He rams it back.

"Move away from the door!"

The pile in the sink has reduced to a smoldering mound of ash. He steps away from the door, turns on the water, and the ash begins to slough down the drain.

The door crashes open and smashes into his

side. A husky man holding a gun falls in with it. The man grabs the counter for balance and lifts his gun to point it at Hans, who raises both arms. The man handcuffs Hans and shoves him out of the bathroom.

Cascades of smoke pour out with them, and Hans recalls a darkwave festival that he and Rachel attended a few months before. One singer had emerged from a cloud of smoke. Hans feels like a performer too. Passengers peer over and around their seats at him. The woman with the kid in 27A points her phone at him, as do an array of other passengers, and he recalls the raised phones at the festival. Hans shakes the hair out of his eyes, and he has the irrational desire to sing the lyrics of the Boy Harsher song, Pain. *What is it that you are doing here? I know. I don't know.*

Maybe this is his moment. He could make up a poem. Something clever and funny and insightful. He could become an internet sensation. Instead, the air marshal shoves him into seat 30A in the back row, and the phones disappear behind seat backs. He imagines his fellow passengers sending out videos of him on social media. News sites could pick them up, interview Prof. Mettles, and add headlines. "Failed Student Arrested After Torching Humiliating Magazine" or "Kafka Prank Takes Down Ph.D. Student." He knows he didn't destroy all of the magazines. Maybe some will become collector's items sold for thousands of dollars on eBay. Not that he'll get any of that money. His father may be so ashamed that he won't allow him in the house. Maybe after a stint in jail, he'll end up living in a tent encampment, plucking half-eaten food out of trash cans. He might turn to drugs, overdose, and one day be found dead, his fetid smell bringing the police to his tent. His epitaph will read, "Here lies Hans Braun. Disreputable. Dishonored. Disgraceful."

A tear slides down his sooty face. A passenger across the aisle takes a photo.

***

Rain splatters Hans' window as the pilot announces that they are entering the skies over Oregon. The kid in seat 27A pokes his head over his seat back and stares at Hans. The boy grips a purple crayon in one hand and a pad of paper in the other. Hans recalls himself at that age. His mother had given him a sketchbook and a mammoth box of crayons at breakfast on the day she died. He had filled it with drawings and stories. Sometimes, as he drew alone at the desk facing his bedroom window, he thought he saw her emerging from the murk of storm clouds outside. He would whisper stories to her, and his mood would lighten. He showed the sketchbook to his father in hopes that the fanciful beasts and imaginings would lift him from his grief, but his father found no joy in the tales. One day, the journal vanished. Hans found it in the kitchen trash under runny eggshells and a mound of wet coffee grounds. He tried to clean it, but it only stunk and moldered until he tossed it in the trash again.

Maybe the time had come for a new journal. The kid peeks over his seat back, and Hans lifts his handcuffed hands, holding one flat like a piece of paper, while he uses the other to pretend he's drawing on it. The kid slides back down in his seat, emerges in the aisle, walks down it, and pauses beside Hans' row.

He hands Hans a few pieces of paper and holds out a box of crayons. "You can pick eight."

"Eight?" Hans says.

"It's the best number in the world."

"For me, it's the worst."

"Maybe you're not looking at it right. My grandma says you can turn every lemon into lemonade."

Hans snorts. A loud embarrassing snort. A snort that changes to a snicker, then to a chuckle, and finally an uncontrollable guffaw. His body bucks and throbs. His face scrunches up, flattens, then scrunches again. His skin flames red. He howls so hard that tears slide down his face. The boy studies him, half-smiling, and Hans recalls the picture on the magazine cover with the Hans in a whirlpool. He is in a whirlpool of laughter. He is that Hans. The idea makes him laugh harder. He laughs so hard that it hurts. He tries to stop, but then is overcome again.

Eventually, in jerks and spasms, the mirth subsides, and he can laugh no more. Hans leans back in his seat, exhausted, cheeks wet, more relaxed than he's been in years, in decades. The boy watches him, and Hans yearns to thank him. The crayons, the paper, the laughter. Three undeserved gifts.

Hans stares into the kid's sweet, hopeful eyes and says, "I'll try."

Acknowledgements

This Deck would have never been assembled without Henry Lien, UCLA instructor, Wu Liu master, and the vector that brought this writing squad together. We further salute J.J. Mongk for combining visual creativity with authorial and creating our cover art and story imagery; Laurel Busby for wielding her fine-toothed editorial comb; and Hardy Griffin of Novel Slices for offering his book formatting services. This Deck is in your hands, thanks to these fine humans. Lastly, we thank you, dear reader, for joining us on the adventure.

Contributors

Kayla Al-Shamma-Jones is a stir-crazy hermit with a vivid imagination and a proclivity towards the bizarre. Her work draws influence from the beloved kooky sci-fi of yore, East Asian magical realism, and literary darlings. In those rare moments when she's not writing, she likes to hang with her super-cool daughter or wrastle with her overactive cats. In 2022, she graduated from the prestigious UCLA Extension Writers' Program with a focus on Novel Writing. She lives in Redondo Beach, California and never leaves the house without her giant black sunhat.

Laurel Busby, an L.A. transplant who grew up in Atlanta, has earned honors for her work from the National Newspaper Association, the California Newspaper Publishers Association, and chapters of the Society of Children's Book Writers and Illustrators. She graduated from the UCLA Extension Writers' Program in 2022 with a focus in creative writing and is currently wrapping up the final draft of her novel, *Amara Rising*, a dramatic mystery set in Ancient Greece.

A. S. Klatt-Diego enjoys escapist stories with strong female leads and queer themes. When not working or spending time with loved ones, she can be found haunting food trucks and coffee shops around the San Francisco Bay Area.

S. L. Johnson's speculative fiction appears in publications like *Antipodean SF*, *The Colored Lens*, *In Another Time* and more. A former NYC Midnight judge, she is currently an editor at *Novel Slices* and is a graduate of the 2023 Wayward Wormhole Workshop. She is originally from the US but is currently based in Sydney, Australia.

Margaret Lê is an Oakland, California based writer whose speculative fiction explores the intersection of the surreal and the everyday. A believer in sustainable urbanism, she draws inspiration from her love of exploring cityscapes on bike, foot, and public transit. Her work invites readers to venture into worlds bathed in whimsy, where the familiar mingles with the strange.

M.C.S. Levine writes speculative fiction influenced by science and nature. Shaping worlds—on Earth and beyond—that envision queer joy and defy dystopian norms fuels M's work. M was raised by a pack of wild books and currently resides on the western edge of the North American continent.

J.J. MONGK is Thai-Chinese growing up in Thailand before moving to LA in 2005. J.J. did not know what to do with his life after almost not getting his Bachelor's in Math. He dabbled around with different hobbies such as stand-up comedy, improv comedy, acting, rock climbing, martial arts, dances, and so on. Influenced by a lot of manga and anime, he is now trying his hand at writing. You can see more of his stuff including silly drawings at jjmongk.com.

Printed in the USA
CPSIA information can be obtained
at www.ICGtesting.com
LVHW091510081124
796065LV00009B/725